The Paper Chase

The Paper Chase

JOHN JAY OSBORN, JR.

HOUGHTON MIFFLIN COMPANY BOSTON 1971

To E.H.S.O.

1970
Official Register of Harvard University
Catalogue for the Law School:

". . . the predominant method of instruction in the Law School is the case method, first developed as a technique for law teaching by Dean Langdell in 1870, and since extensively employed in virtually all American law schools. The case method is a realistic method which uses the careful examination of judicial opinions as a focus for study and as a starting point for classroom discussion . . . The case method also introduces the student to the analytical techniques which lawyers use to sort the relevant from the irrelevant, separate reasoning from rationalization, and distinguish solid principle from speculation. The case method is a flexible instrument . . ."

". . . citizens who take it upon themselves to do unusual actions which attract the attention of the police should be careful to bring these actions into one of the recognized categories of crimes and offenses for it is intolerable that the police should be put to the pains of inventing reasons for finding them undesirable . . . It is not for me to say what offense the appellant has committed, but I am satisfied that he has committed some offense, for which he has been most properly punished."

— Fog, L. J., *Rex* v. *Haddock* in the Court of Criminal Appeal (Haddock, Misl. Cas. C. Law 31. Herbert, Ed; 1927.)

FALL ❦❦

In the few days between arrival at Harvard Law School and the first classes, there are rumors. And stories. About being singled out, made to show your stuff.

Mostly, they're about people who made some terrible mistake. Couldn't answer a question right.

One concerns a boy who did a particularly bad job. His professor called him down to the front of the class, up to the podium, gave the student a dime and said, loudly:

"Go call your mother, and tell her you'll never be a lawyer."

Sometimes the story ends here, but the way I heard it, the crushed student bowed his head and limped slowly back through the one hundred and fifty students in the class. When he got to the door, his anger exploded. He screamed:

"You're a son of a bitch, Kingsfield."

"That's the first intelligent thing you've said," Kingsfield replied. "Come back. Perhaps I've been too hasty."

1

Professor Kingsfield, who should have been reviewing the cases he would offer his first class of the year, stared down from the window forming most of the far wall of his second story office in Langdell Hall and watched the students walking to class.

He was panting. Professor Kingsfield had just done forty push-ups on his green carpet. His vest was pulled tight around his small stomach and it seemed, each time his heart heaved, the buttons would give way.

A pyramid-shaped wooden box, built for keeping time during piano lessons, was ticking on his desk and he stopped its pendulum. Professor Kingsfield did his push-ups in four-four time.

His secretary knocked on the door and reminded him that if he didn't get moving he'd be late. She paused in the doorway, watching his heaving chest. Since Crane had broken his hip in a fall from the lecture platform, Professor Kingsfield was the oldest active member of the Harvard Law School faculty.

He noticed her concern and smiled, picked up the casebook he had written thirty years before, threw his jacket over his shoulder and left the office.

Hart tried to balance the three huge casebooks under one arm, and with the other hold up his little map. He really needed two hands to carry the casebooks — combined, they were more than fifteen inches thick, with smooth dust jackets that tended to make the middle book slide out — and he stumbled along, trying to find Langdell North and avoid bumping into another law student.

Everything would have been easy if he had known which direction was North. He had figured out that the dotted lines didn't represent paths, but instead tunnels, somewhere under his feet, connecting the classrooms, the library, the dorms and the eating hall in Harkness. He knew that the sharp red lines were the paths — little asphalt tracks winding along through the maze of granite buildings.

Some of the buildings were old. Langdell was old: a three story dark stone building, built in neoclassical renaissance. It stretched out for a block in front of and behind him, with the library on the third floor. Hart had been circling it for ten minutes trying to find an entrance that would lead to his classroom.

The other buildings he'd passed were more modern but

in an attempt to compromise with Langdell had been given the library's worst features. They were tall concrete rectangles, broken by large dark windows, woven around Langdell like pillboxes, guarding the perimeter of the monolith. It seemed that everything was interconnected, not only by the tunnels, but also by bridges which sprung out from the second and third floors of Langdell like spider legs, gripping the walls of the outposts.

Hart took a reading on the sun, trying to remember from his Boy Scout days where it rose. He absolutely refused to ask anyone the way. He disliked being a first year student, disliked not knowing where things were. Most of all, he disliked feeling unorganized, and he was terribly unorganized on this first day of classes. He couldn't read his map, he couldn't carry his casebooks. His glasses had fallen down over his nose, and he didn't have a free hand to lift them up.

He had expected to have these troubles, and knew from experience that he wouldn't want to ask directions. Thus, he had allowed a full twenty minutes to find the classroom. His books were slowly sliding forward from under his arm, and he wondered if he should reconsider his vow never to buy a briefcase.

He moved into a flow of red books, tucked on top of other casebooks. Red. His contracts book was red. He followed the flow to one of the stone entrances to Langdell, up the granite steps. In the hallway, groups of students pushed against each other, as they tried to squeeze through the classroom door. Every now and then books hit the floor when students bumped. A contagious feeling of tension hung in the corridor. People were overly polite or overly rude. Hart pulled his books to his chest, let his map drop to the floor, and started pushing toward the red door of the classroom.

*   *   *

Most of the first year students, in anticipation of their first class at the Harvard Law School, were already seated as Professor Kingsfield, at exactly five minutes past nine, walked purposefully through the little door behind the lecture platform. He put his books and notes down on the wooden lectern and pulled out the seating chart. One hundred and fifty names and numbers: the guide to the assigned classroom seats. He put the chart on the lectern, unbuttoned his coat, exposing the gold chain across his vest, and gripped the smooth sides of the stand, feeling for the indentations he had worn into the wood. He did not allow his eyes to meet those of any student — his face had a distant look similar to the ones in the thirty or so large gilt-framed portraits of judges and lawyers that hung around the room.

Professor Kingsfield was at ease with the room's high ceiling, thick beams, tall thin windows. Though he knew the room had mellowed to the verge of decay, he disliked the new red linoleum bench tops. They hid the mementos carved by generations of law students, and accented the fact that the wooden chairs were losing their backs, the ceiling peeling, and the institutional light brown paint on the walls turning the color of mud. He could have taught in one of the new classrooms with carpets and programmed acoustics designed to hold less than the full quota of a hundred and fifty students. But he had taught in this room for thirty years, and felt at home.

At exactly ten past nine, Professor Kingsfield picked a name from the seating chart. The name came from the left side of the classroom. Professor Kingsfield looked off to the right, his eyes following one of the curving benches to where it ended by the window.

Without turning, he said crisply, "Mr. Hart, will you recite the facts of *Hawkins* versus *McGee?*"

6

When Hart, seat 259, heard his name, he froze. Caught unprepared, he simply stopped functioning. Then he felt his heart beat faster than he could ever remember its beating and his palms and arms break out in sweat.

Professor Kingsfield rotated slowly until he was staring down at Hart. The rest of the class followed Kingsfield's eyes.

"I have got your name right?" Kingsfield asked. "You are Mr. Hart?" He spoke evenly, filling every inch of the hall.

A barely audible voice floated back: "Yes, my name is Hart."

"Mr. Hart, you're not speaking loud enough. Will you speak up?"

Hart repeated the sentence, no louder than before. He tried to speak loudly, tried to force the air out of his lungs with a deep push, tried to make his words come out with conviction. He could feel his face whitening, his lower lip beat against his upper. He couldn't speak louder.

"Mr. Hart, will you stand?"

After some difficulty, Hart found, to his amazement, he was on his feet.

"Now, Mr. Hart, will you give us the case?"

Hart had his book open to the case: he had been informed by the student next to him that a notice on the bulletin board listed *Hawkins* v. *McGee* as part of the first day's assignment in contracts. But Hart had not known about the bulletin board. Like most of the students, he had assumed that the first lecture would be an introduction.

His voice floated across the classroom: "I . . . I haven't read the case. I only found out about it just now."

Kingsfield walked to the edge of the platform.

"Mr. Hart, I will myself give you the facts of the case.

Hawkins versus *McGee* is a case in contract law, the subject of our study. A boy burned his hand by touching an electric wire. A doctor who wanted to experiment in skin grafting asked to operate on the hand, guaranteeing that he would restore the hand 'one hundred percent.' Unfortunately, the operation failed to produce a healthy hand. Instead, it produced a hairy hand. A hand not only burned, but covered with dense matted hair.

"Now, Mr. Hart, what sort of damages do you think the doctor should pay?"

Hart reached into his memory for any recollections of doctors. There were squeaks from the seats as members of the class adjusted their positions. Hart tried to remember the summation he had just heard, tried to think about it in a logical sequence. But all his mental energy had been expended in pushing back shock waves from the realization that, though Kingsfield had appeared to be staring at a boy on the other side of the room, he had in fact called out the name Hart. And there was the constant strain of trying to maintain his balance because the lecture hall sloped toward the podium at the center, making him afraid that if he fainted he would fall on the student in front of him.

Hart said nothing.

"As you remember, Mr. Hart, this was a case involving a doctor who promised to restore an injured hand."

That brought it back. Hart found that if he focused on Kingsfield's face, he could imagine there was no one else in the room. A soft haze formed around the face. Hart's eyes were watering, but he could speak.

"There was a promise to fix the hand back the way it was before," Hart said.

Kingsfield interrupted: "And what in fact was the result of the operation?"

8

"The hand was much worse than when it was just burned . . ."

"So the man got less than he was promised, even less than he had when the operation started?"

Kingsfield wasn't looking at Hart now. He had his hands folded across his chest. He faced out, catching as many of the class's glances as he could.

"Now, Mr. Hart," Kingsfield said, "how should the court measure the damages?"

"The difference between what he was promised, a new hand, and what he got, a worse hand?" Hart asked.

Kingsfield stared off to the right, picked a name from the seating chart.

"Mr. Pruit, perhaps you can tell the class if we should give the boy the difference between what he was promised and what he got, as Mr. Hart suggests, or the difference between what he got, and what he had."

Hart fell back into his seat. He blinked, trying to erase the image of Kingsfield suspended in his mind. He couldn't. The lined white skin, the thin rusty lips grew like a balloon until the image seemed to actually press against his face, shutting off everything else in the classroom.

Hart blinked again, felt for his pen and tried to focus on his clean paper. His hand shook, squiggling a random line. Across the room, a terrified, astonished boy with a beard and wire-rimmed glasses was slowly talking about the hairy hand.

2

HART HAD BEEN WORKING for more than five hours in his concrete dorm room just large enough for a desk, a chair and a bed. He kept on only the desk light. It made the room seem larger and blocked out distractions. Gradually, he had locked into the work, oblivious to time and the physical action of turning pages.

His door opened, a boy peered in and said something. Hart didn't move, didn't even hear the question. The boy closed the door and sat on the bed, two feet away. The sight of Hart completely into his work, with one light on, made the boy feel reverent. It was a picture to put with the dark faces in gilt frames hanging in the classrooms in Langdell.

Then Hart knew someone was in the room. It came slowly: first just sensing he was losing contact with his casebook, and then, more quickly, the realization that there was breathing in the room, that the breathing was not his, that someone was there. It passed through his mind like cue cards. He saw Ford on the bed.

"How long have you been there?" Hart said. Ford was the only student Hart had met in the first two weeks. Ford had introduced himself after the first contracts class and the fact that it was Ford, not Hart, who had taken the initiative gave Hart a slight feeling of superiority.

"I just came in," Ford said. "I knocked, but you didn't hear it. I came to ask you to join my study group."

"Study group?" Hart said.

"You'll hear about study groups pretty soon. Groups of first year students get together, review the classwork, the casebooks. They make outlines and then share them with the group. It helps at exam time."

"All right," Hart said, "I'll join the group." He squirmed around in his chair and looked away from Ford.

"Just think about it," Ford said. "You don't have to make up your mind."

Hart didn't want to think about it. "I'll join," he said. "It doesn't make any difference to me."

10

Ford smiled and stood up.

"Have you gotten a lot done?" he said. "Are you planning to study all night?"

"No," Hart said, "I'm really finished." There were other things he wanted to say. He wanted to say thank you. He wanted Ford to stay with him for a while.

"Want to get drunk?" Ford asked.

"I had three roommates during my freshman year in college. One was a genius, one was crazy and one was inconsequential and kept to himself," Hart said.

"It sounds like a fairy tale," Ford whispered. He was woozy. The bourbon had gone to his head and now he lay stretched out on the bed, staring at the ceiling. He let Hart's words fall over him like music, lulling him to sleep. It was good that Hart was talking, that the wine had unlocked him. Ford wanted that.

"The genius surprised us the first week. We were all trying to write our first papers. It scared the hell out of us. I've never worked so hard on anything. But the genius was cool: he didn't do anything at all. We figured he didn't give a damn.

"The night before the papers were due, he swung into action. Sat down and started typing, faster than I ever saw anyone type. He started about eleven and finished at one. We hung around his door, wondering what the hell would happen.

"When he finished, he had twenty-five neatly typed pages. He'd proofread them as they came over the top of the typewriter. I got a C minus on my paper and the genius got his back with a note asking him to continue his work in English Literature for the sake of future generations. I had to work for a year before I got an A on a paper."

Hart sank down in his seat, staring at the light in the ceiling.

"What about the crazy roommate?" Ford asked.

"He was fixed on inviting his high school sweetheart up for a college weekend. He'd write her letters, tell us she was coming any day. But he didn't have any money and his parents wouldn't send him any. One day his girl told him to get lost."

Hart's voice was sinking low, just a trickle sliding to Ford.

"We were lonely during the first weeks. When there were dances, we could hear music through the window and see couples walking under the trees. One night, two couples sat down on the steps outside the dorm. The genius and I were on the third floor, listening to records. The crazy roommate came in with a wastebasket filled with water. He wanted us to help him dump it on the couples. We told him he was crazy, but he did it anyway. There was a tremendous scream. Then these two huge guys were in our room, saying they were going to beat the shit out of us. We told them we didn't have anything to do with it, but we didn't want to tell them right out who did. The crazy roommate had hidden in his bedroom, and the genius told the guys that if they knocked on the door, they'd get some valuable information.

"So they knocked, and the crazy roommate came out dressed in his pajamas, saying why the hell couldn't he get any sleep around the dorm."

"Jesus," Ford said.

"This made us hate him because he'd put us in the position of getting the shit kicked out of us. We had thought he was pathetic, his girl friend and all that, but now we saw he was dangerous. Anyway, then the soap in the bathroom started to disappear. I'd go in for a shower, turn on the water, reach into the soap dish to lather up and find it empty. I didn't say anything about it, but when it happened to the genius, he got upset.

"He set up this plan. I invited the crazy roommate into my room. By that time he was pretty anxious to make friends with someone, anyone. He felt pretty good about it. As soon as he came in, the genius went into the crazy roommate's room. The soap was hidden in his socks. We confronted him, but he denied it all, and then we couldn't find the soap in his socks. The genius went wild: took the crazy roommate by the neck, forced him on the floor, dug his fingernails into his skin. Finally he blubbered out that the soap was hidden in his shoes."

"God," Ford whispered, "he was crazy as hell."

"Yes," Hart said. "But that's not the end. I mean, he was *really* crazy. About three in the morning, he came into my room and told me he didn't care what the genius thought of him, but that he treasured my friendship. He started crying. Can you imagine what it's like having one of your roommates crying and begging you to be his friend? I almost threw up."

"What did you do?" Ford said. "What did you say?"

"Nothing. I couldn't think of anything. Anyway, he left school and that finished it."

I've been to college and I know. The things you hear about don't really happen, or if they do, they aren't interesting. Sex, riots, drugs: no one tries to hide them.

What really happens has been happening for ever so long. People kill themselves. They hang themselves, jump out of windows, turn on the gas. Sometimes they blow their brains out with guns.

Behind every good college are a hundred boys who killed themselves.

It's very unpredictable. My father is head of the history department. One day his best student — shy, earnest, likable — called up to say he had just killed himself. He said it very matter-of-factly: "I just killed myself." He had cut his throat. So Dad rushed over in the middle of the night, and found the boy, still holding the phone, with the big blood vessel in his neck cut out with a razor blade.

3

ASHELEY GROVE, Mrs. Kevin Brooks, was a very simple girl. She thought of herself that way and regarded it as a compliment.

It was her night out and she was sitting in the Cambridge Center for Adult Education listening to a very old professor, who looked as if he might collapse at any moment, talk about medieval history. Asheley didn't believe half of what he said, but she liked listening to the stories. The professor was talking about Pietro di Murrhone, the "Holy Hermit" who came down from his cave to become Pope Celestine V, in 1294, and abdicated after five months, expressing doubts about his own salvation as a result of the experience.

Asheley wasn't really serious about medieval history and she had been afraid to come to the class, thinking that she would have trouble getting to know the other students. As it happened, most of the people were like herself: wives of law or business school students, conservatively dressed quiet girls who had completed two or three years of college. They'd managed to turn the class into a social club. When the lecture ended they would have coffee together and talk about what life was going to be like when their husbands graduated.

Most of the girls were envious of Asheley. Most had to work. They didn't have Asheley's father, who was paying for Kevin's education at the law school. They didn't have the time Asheley did to think about the babies they were going to have and the houses they were going to decorate.

After coffee, Asheley said good-bye and began her meandering walk home. She could have gone by a more direct route but she kept to the lighted streets. She didn't like walking home alone. She wished Kevin had continued his practice of walking her there and picking her up. In fact, she'd tried to insist on it and the result had been a real fight. Kevin was upset. He was studying very hard.

Once she had tried to visit him in the big library in Langdell Hall. She had made some cookies and wrapped them in tinfoil. But the dark gray building was too imposing. She'd made it into the lobby and then she'd met a group of students. She couldn't do it after that, knowing that there would be more students upstairs, and that she'd have to search among them for Kevin. She'd hidden the tinfoil package in her coat and fled.

She felt more comfortable in the apartment. She'd decorated it, and she liked its warmth and closeness — the way it was protected by the apartments around it.

Ahead, waiting in the street for the bus, Asheley saw seven or eight teen-agers. The group was playing a game that looked like tag. Perhaps they were just having fun touching each other. Asheley moved away from them, toward the buildings.

As Asheley passed, one of the girls, dressed in a fringed coat that came down over her shoes, pulled on her shoulder.

"Hey, lady," the girl said, smiling from behind the mass of curly hair around her face, "give me twenty cents for the bus, O.K.?"

Asheley shuddered at the girl's touch. She pulled away, jerked backward and slapped the girl's hand down. The others in the group watched Asheley as she backed away from them down the street.

In ten minutes she was home. She sprinted up her stairs. Kevin was in the living room, bent down over his books,

16

flipping the pages like a machine. She dropped her things on the couch, threw her arms around him and put her face down on his neck. His hand jerked forward over his notes, twisting a line down the center of the page.

"What the hell did you do that for?" he said, dislodging her. She turned sideways to him, looking meek and ashamed.

"I'm just happy to see you," she said, and came forward again, reaching out for him. He lay down on the sofa, and stuck his head into a pillow.

"Oh, Kevin, don't put your feet on the sofa," Asheley said, sitting down and rubbing his back.

"Jesus Christ, you made me mess up my notes. Do you want me to work or not?"

He was so perfect looking. His blond hair, blue eyes. It melted her. She wanted to touch his face, trace the lines with her finger.

"Let's go to bed," she said. "If you work harder, you'll hurt yourself." She slid a hand around his neck and kissed him.

4

"Look," Toombs said, "you guys have any questions? Anything else you want to know about the dorm? The rules? Don't worry about the rules — screw, anything you want. I don't give a shit. I'm not an advisor, I just sort of watch the dorm."

Hart shifted, getting comfortable on Toombs' bed, wondering if Toombs was really supposed to watch over the dorm or if he'd made it all up. Ford was in the corner looking through last year's law school yearbook.

"I guess I've covered everything I'm supposed to tell you,"

Toombs said. "Thanks for coming. I'm inviting everyone in the dorm in for these talks. Wish I'd got to you sooner."

Hart started to rise.

"Oh yes," Toombs said quickly, "the only second and third year students around here are failures. Don't listen to them. They still live in the dorm because they couldn't find a roommate, or Cambridge scared them. They never leave the law school, except to take a taxi to the airport. Their skin is pale from spending so much time in the tunnels."

"Why did you stay?" Hart asked. Toombs didn't look like a failure. He looked like what a lawyer should look like: a good suit, vest, a little wrinkled so you knew he'd been working.

"Me?" Toombs said. "I get an allowance for watching the dorm, for watching you guys." He started to unbutton his vest and noticed that Hart was staring at the yellow lines set in the dark blue silk like stays in a corset.

"That," Toombs said, "is what getting a job will do for you. Congealed sweat. It costs too much to clean it after each interview."

Ford looked up from the book.

"One more thing," Toombs said. "All that stuff about grades is true. You've got to work like hell. Next time you think about bugging out of the library, don't."

"Christ," Ford said under his breath.

"You think I'm kidding? You think I'd joke about grades? You try getting a job if you don't have them. Either you've got to look right, or you've got to have the grades."

Hart was thinking that you didn't wear professional clothes unless you were good.

"I was supposed to do well," Toombs said, "but I choked up. Like in the interview today. My only chance was to

18

stall on the grades, while I showed how much experience I had. It didn't work. It's all stacked against you, if you don't have the grades."

"What are you interviewing for?" Ford asked.

"A job in New York." Toombs nervously ran his hand through his curly black hair. "I need the money. Don't think you've got it made because you go to Harvard. You can't wear Harvard on a sign around your neck. Like I said, you've got to look good, or have the grades." He stubbed out his cigarette and hitched up his feet on the lower rung of his chair.

"Well, thanks," Hart said, starting to rise again.

"I walk in, the room is dark as hell, just this one light bulb, about fifteen watts, hanging from a string. And the wind blows the light bulb so it throws weird shadows all over the room. They plan it that way so you can't hide things."

"Well," Ford said, "we don't have to worry about that yet. Thanks." He looked at Hart.

"Either of you from New York?" Toombs said. "New York firms hate to hire people from New York. I'm from New York. They want people from the South. They don't have to teach them manners. Anyway, this fat man is sitting behind a desk. He says to me, 'Mr. Toombs, what courses have you liked at Harvard?' Then he leans back, and the bulb sways in the wind, hanging strange reflections over his glasses so I can't see his eyes. You know, like he's wearing those sunglasses that have mirrors on the front? He just wants to know my grades. That's what the question is for. I stall him. I say I liked property. New York firms always like property law."

"I hope you get a job," Hart said.

"Then the fat man leans over, out of the shadows, and says right out, 'How did you do in property?' I got a D in property, and if I tell him that the interview is over. My only chance is to keep the fat man guessing. I say, 'Well, I did O.K.'

"The fat man slides back into the shadows and I think I've done it, that he thinks I'm just modest, that he thinks I did real well. I mean, it makes me feel good because this is life or death.

"But I see he's peeking a look at his watch, back in the dark, and I know he wants to be on a plane home with a drink. He swings right in front of my face and says, 'Toombs, *exactly* how did you do in property?' I feel like he's shot me. It caught me off guard in the dark and all."

"Thanks for telling us about grades," Hart said. "We'll remember."

"I didn't give the fat bastard the satisfaction of knowing how bad I did. I knew he didn't like the way I looked, they don't like curly hair, and telling him I got a B minus average would have sealed it, made him feel objective. So I spit out: 'I don't remember how I did.' It'll keep him awake nights, thinking maybe I was on Law Review."

Ford and Hart had reached the door. Toombs seemed to be contemplating things.

"We'll remember the rules," Ford said.

"You see, you don't want to go through that shit. So don't slack off on the studying. That's the main thing to remember around the dorm. That's the main rule." He saw they were halfway out the door.

"I don't know," he called. "Maybe you've just got it or you don't. Maybe that's the way it is. Remember I'm here to answer your questions. Just ask. Remember I'm the only third year student you can trust. Talk to me."

In the hall, walking back to their room, Hart and Ford were quiet. Outside Hart's door, Ford smiled weakly and shook his head.

5

THE STUDY GROUP sat around an oblong table in one of the small discussion rooms off the lounge on the first floor of the dormitory.

"The only sensible thing is to divide up the courses," Ford said. "Each person do an outline. Then at the end of the year we have them Xeroxed and exchange them."

"I want property," Bell said, the words lumbering out of him. Bell was big — he took up nearly the whole end of the table. The way he talked made words seem big too. He opened his mouth wide.

"There's no guarantee that we will all be here in the spring," Anderson said, ignoring Bell. "After all, some of us might be drafted, or have nervous breakdowns. I think we should research the incidence of nervous breakdowns."

"I'm gonna take property," Bell said.

Kevin was stubbing out a cigarette. Before the smoke died, he lit another. Each movement was perfectly balanced, practiced.

"I've already started to outline property," O'Connor said, flexing his backbone, and then snapping up to give himself a few extra inches. Even so, his mustache barely reached Bell's shoulder.

"Hart, don't you think this is the logical thing to do?" Ford said. "To divide up the courses?" Hart nodded slowly.

"All right," Ford said. "Let's divide the courses up."

"We've divided them," Bell said. "I'm taking property.

That course was made for me. I need it. Real estate law is where the action is." His eyes lit up. He made property sound like a whole school.

"I think we should talk about who gets which course," O'Connor said. "Maybe we should draw lots. Like I said, I've started to outline property."

"Forget it," Bell growled. His hand turned into a fist, and the veins of his wrist popped out of the flesh. O'Connor looked at Ford.

"Listen, Bell," Ford said.

Anderson cut in. "Bell, try to think of this in terms of maximum utility. Apply some logic. Each course is weighted equally as far as your average is concerned. Strive for the highest average you can attain. Treat all your courses as of equal importance."

"I've already decided," Bell said. "They're not equal."

Anderson looked out the window. Then everyone looked away from Bell.

"Oh hell," Bell said slowly. His fist relaxed and he inspected the table. "I don't know. My father is in property law. I know that stuff."

"Go ahead and take property," O'Connor said. His little face rounded out in a smile. "If you like it, you'll do a better job. I can outline something else."

"Anderson," Ford said, "which course do you want?"

Anderson adjusted his black glasses.

"It's not important to me," he said. "I've already made out a studying schedule to the end of the year, dividing my time equally among all courses. I'll outline anything."

"Kevin?" Ford said.

Kevin stubbed out his cigarette, half burned. He drew back in his chair. His voice came out high-pitched.

"I don't know," he said. "I don't know which course I'll be best at."

"You shouldn't necessarily outline your best course," Anderson said, glancing at Bell. "Perhaps your overall average will improve if you outline your worst."

"I don't know which is my worst," Kevin said.

Kevin's nervousness, a fingernail on slate, sketched lines on Hart's mind.

"All right," Ford said, "Hart, which do you want?"

"Contracts," Hart said, blinking.

"I'll take criminal law," Ford said. "You guys who haven't decided — you can divide up the rest any way you want."

6

HART FINISHED HIS WORK about one-thirty most nights, and afterward he wrote a letter. Sometimes to his parents. Sometimes to his girl back in Minnesota. Tonight when he tried to write, the letter didn't come. He bent over his pad, conjuring up visions, but all he could see were the pages of the large casebooks on his desk.

The cool autumn air slid in through the window, inviting him out into the absolute quiet. He pulled on a Pendleton shirt and opened the door to his room. In the long corridor, the doors of most rooms were at least partly open, anticipating the ring of the one pay phone. Standing across from it, outside his door, Hart heard pages turning, pens quietly marking up the casebooks, abstracting cases for easy reference the next day.

Maybe he should go back. In torts, the methodical German was proceeding down rows, calling people in order.

He was five seats away from Hart. Would he ask five questions in the fifty minutes of class? Hart pushed it out of his mind. He cursed the linoleum tile floors which echoed his footsteps.

Outside he saw the rows of windows, actually saw faces bent down over books, etched by the desk light into the blackness of the rest of the room.

He crossed the grassy yard in front of Langdell — it looked like the Escorial, a mad black shroud — and walked away from the law school and the college, losing himself in the small Cambridge streets.

He had no idea where he was going and after five minutes, no idea where he was except for a vague feeling that the law school was somewhere off to the right. Down a side street the cramped three story buildings opened up into a small park crisscrossed with asphalt paths. He stopped and scouted the clearing. The park's dull lamps were warm. He'd cross, move into the open.

He had thought he was alone. Behind him came quick taps, footsteps, light and moving fast toward him. A figure, closing in, coming to him, not past. Impossible, he thought, not turning again, I don't know anyone.

He expected the girl to pass quickly, but as she pulled abreast, her hand took his.

"Do you mind? Just to the street. There's a pervert following me."

From just under a lamp, Hart peered into the darkness. Rounding a corner in the path was a man. His eyes met Hart's and with a squeal, the pervert vanished into the trees.

"At least he's pulled his pants up," the girl said. "He looks better in pants."

He walked her to the edge of the park. She was small,

compact, and he felt protective. Could he go home with her? Could he go to bed with her? Could he run away with her?

He asked if he could see her home. A smile, nothing else, and they walked on, she guiding him by holding his arm, through the small streets, lined with trees, the old wooden frame houses painted in drab colors with white trim.

In front of one of these houses Hart said good-bye and turned to go. Then he realized he didn't even know her name, or which apartment was hers. She was already on the stairs. Even on the sidewalk, he could hear the stairs creak and then a door open. He watched for a sign, and on the third floor a green light went on.

Marking the window, he left for the dorm. Now he could taste the night. It was his friend, slowly uncovering Cambridge, showing him special little things as he walked. He wanted to smile at someone, but there was no one on the streets. He even looked for a policeman to wave at, but he saw only the houses.

Of course, Hart did not write any letters that night. Nor the next. From then on he wrote grudgingly, avoiding anything that might bring probes into what his life was really like. He wrote, "Yes, things are fine. I'm learning a lot. Turning into a real lawyer, and I enjoy the law." He tried to throw his parents and his girl off the track. "Nothing happens here," he wrote. "We sit in the dorm at night and study, worrying about grades," which was mostly true. He wrote, "I don't have time to think of anything but law school," which wasn't.

Two days later, he retraced his steps. He turned down the dead-end street her house was on, walking fast on the opposite side. He glanced up at her window as he passed, saw the green light, turned around at the end of the street and headed back toward the apartment.

The stairs swayed under him. There were footprints in mud that must have been tracked in last winter. On the third floor, he found only one door. It didn't fit its frame. Dull light filtered out around it, along with the quiet music of guitar, dulcimer and pipe.

He stepped back, shaking himself loose, getting calm. The banister quivered with his touch. He looked over, wondering what to grab if it collapsed. Then he knocked hard, three huge swipes at the door to cover his nervousness, and stepped back, thinking maybe it was forward to come so soon.

She came to the door buttoning up the last buttons on a red shirt as faded as her blue jeans.

"I was walking by and saw your light," he said. It was one of his few attempts at a lie. She smiled, not sure whether he was being sarcastic.

"I know you, the pervert," she said, holding the door open.

He stepped into the living room. Chinese paper lamps hung from the ceiling near a low sofa with a paisley print thrown over it. The green light came from a door in the corner, and through it he saw an open window and a bed set on the floor. The musty air seemed to lie in layers. It was too dark to make out the designs of a woven cloth ripping away from nails that pegged it to the far wall.

"It's nice to have visitors," she said.

She sprawled on a pillow facing Hart. He put his coat on the sofa and sat down beside it, leaning against the wall. She wasn't as pretty as he had thought. Perhaps he'd been improving her in his mind. Her hair was thick and full, laced in different shades of brown. It fell in bunches almost to her waist. Nothing stood out, except shining below her ears were tiny earrings — gold circles the size of dimes that swung when her head moved.

He wanted to talk. Wanted to tell her the things that had happened since he came to Cambridge. About not having done his work for tomorrow. About not being able to write letters home. About the study group. He wished she'd ask where he went to school, and then reach into him, bring it all out.

Instead, they talked about books. Mostly, she talked. Asking his preference in things he'd never heard of, explaining subtle variations among authors he'd never read.

He was frustrated by his lack of force, ashamed by his cowardice. Why couldn't he direct the conversation? As he watched her, his body began to weaken, slowly soften. He felt she must feel it too. His mind began to move in visions. A mythical Hart crossing the room, putting a tentative hand in her hair and with the other laying her across the pillow. Nodding thoughtfully as they stretched flat, the pillow under her hips.

"Would you like to drive?" she said.

His mind came back to the room. She was watching him as if she knew everything there was to know.

"There are some good roads about twenty minutes away. It's good to drive at night. There's nothing on the road and the leaves are falling."

The old Porsche looked like a German army helmet, the headlights like holes cut in the rim for eyes. She drove fast, faster than Hart could ever remember driving. He thought about asking her to slow down, or asking to drive himself, but he didn't. What the hell, he thought, it's just this once, if I die, I die. Giving himself up to the speed and the wind, he could talk.

"I don't know . . . I got completely turned on, sitting with you in the room," he said. "If we hadn't gone out for a drive, I would have tried to sleep with you."

She spun the car around a corner. They were in the country now. The road was narrow, no center line, and the car drifted over to the left side, almost brushing the bushes that bent down from the bank. The trees on either side fell together in the wind and touched over the top of the car.

"I know," she said. "That's why I thought we should drive. I didn't want to hurt you."

"You wouldn't have done it?" Hart said. "Do you think *that* would have hurt me?"

"I'm not so condescending that I think the refusal would have hurt you. But if you'd tried, I might have kicked you in the balls. That would have hurt you." She locked her arms straight, pushing herself back into the seat, and laughed.

"Let me ask you something." She slowed the car down to fifty, and looked at Hart very seriously. "Why did you decide to go to law school?"

7

FOR SEVERAL WEEKS, Hart had been preparing to enter a new echelon in the classroom structure. Class had quickly divided into three factions. One was composed of those who sat in the back of the room. They had forever given up sitting in their assigned seats and preparing the cases. They knew they would not make Law Review and had decided it was worthless to reach for anything below. Released from the constant threat of having questions directed to them, they laughed and talked while the class progressed. But it was an uneasy existence, possibly only because the professors respected this truce and would not try to ferret out a student from the anonymous group at the back. And it was degrading when the professor, knowing full well that the student was not sitting in his seat but was in the back, would call out the student's name, lingering over the silence, driving home the fact that he was a coward.

The second group were the students who, though they did not raise their hands and volunteer answers, would attempt a response when called upon. They made no pretense of ease, and lived in admitted constant fear.

The last group, the elite, the upper echelon, were the volunteers. They raised their hands in class: they thrust themselves forward into the fray. It wasn't that they were any smarter than anyone else. They weren't, or at least most of them weren't. But they had courage. They never had to worry about being called on because the professors tried to divide the class time among all the students. And beyond that, in several cases, they had achieved the ultimate recognition. The professors knew their names — knew them on sight.

Hart began his preparations carefully. He answered questions to himself, trying to beat the time of the student who was actually answering. He kept a record of the times his answer matched the one the professor ultimately gave his blessing to. Gradually his record improved, and he was frequently able to guess precisely what the professor was leading toward.

Finally he felt that his record was good enough and chose a section of his contracts course, about a week in advance of the current materials. He carefully prepared an outline.

Sometimes he was amazed at what he was doing. Why didn't he just answer, put it on the line? Why was he so concerned about answering the question correctly? He knew that the emulation of the third group came from the mere fact that they answered the question and had nothing to do with whether they answered the question right. And why did he keep his preparations secret, especially from Ford? He chose Monday for the attempt. Over the weekend he reviewed his outline, wrote out endless lists of possible questions and tried to get some sleep.

Class started unexpectedly. Kingsfield lectured for twenty minutes, summarizing the material they had been discussing through the previous week. Hart heard nothing of the lecture. He copied Kingsfield's words in jagged pen strokes, sometimes cutting through his paper. Finally Kingsfield turned to the first case in the new section, *Carlill* v. *Carbolic Smoke Ball Co.* Without looking for a raised hand, he picked a name from the seating chart.

"Mr. Farranti, could you give us the facts of *Carbolic Smoke Ball?*"

Hart's hand shot up. He was sitting directly below Farranti, and as Farranti bent forward to answer, Hart's hand was thrust in front of Farranti's mouth, two inches away from his lips, which twisted up at the corners in astonishment as he swallowed the words he was about to reply with.

Recovering, Farranti gave the facts of the case while Hart occupied himself drawing lines on his paper, his hand completely out of control.

Carlill v. *Carbolic Smoke Ball Co.* was not difficult to relate to the class. The defendants entered an advertisement in the *Pall Mall Gazette*, in November of 1891, stating:

£100 reward will be paid by the Carbolic Smoke Ball Company to any person who contracts the increasing epidemic influenza, colds, or any disease caused by taking cold, after having used the ball three times daily for two weeks according to the printed directions supplied with each ball . . .

During the last epidemic of influenza many thousand carbolic smoke balls were sold as preventives against this disease, and in no ascertained case was the disease contracted by those using the carbolic smoke ball.

On the strength of this advertisement, a Mrs. Carlill bought a smoke ball, used it diligently, according to the instructions, until she developed influenza.

When Farranti had finished, Kingsfield asked him for the court's reasons in finding in favor of Mrs. Carlill. Farranti did not reply immediately but several of the regular participants raised their hands. That stimulated Farranti into action: "She had fulfilled the conditions of the offer. The bargain was complete."

Kingsfield addressed his next question to the class. "Ah, but was there a bargain here? Was there an actual communication between the parties? Did she not have an obligation to notify the company if she had accepted their offer?"

Hart tensed. He had not reached any final conclusion about the proper answer to the question. But time was running out. He might not get another chance. As if he were reaching up for a light cord in a dark room, he raised his hand and Kingsfield, glancing up from the seating chart, called his name.

"It's obvious that notice is not important here. The offer requires no notice, it requires no personal communication. What is important is consideration. You can only have a binding contract when each party gives something to the other. Did Mrs. Carlill give anything to the company? The company argued that Mrs. Carlill, in using the ball, did nothing for them. All they were interested in was the sale.

The answer to that is, of course, that the company benefits from the sale itself. But beyond this, consideration does not necessarily, in all cases, have to pass *to* the other party. Mrs. Carlill suffered the inconvenience of having to use the ball. She gave something up, even if it did not pass to the other party."

It was a good answer. Even though it was not a complete analysis, or a hard question. Hart had surprised himself. He stared back at Kingsfield, concentrating on his eyes. His words were more than an attempt to solve the problem, more than an attempt to learn the law. He wanted his words to hit Kingsfield physically, like spit.

When class ended, Hart sat still while the students around him picked up their books and put on their coats. He felt that none of them mattered, that this class belonged only to him and Kingsfield. He had the completely unrealistic idea that somehow Kingsfield had known beforehand about this day, about the preparations, about the significance of his raising his hand.

He picked up his papers and casebooks, took a deep breath and started to leave the now empty room. Jesus Christ, he thought, this is a goddamned dance.

8

HART SAT on the grass at Fresh Pond. Children were playing, throwing a Frisbee. Susan had gone walking around the point. It was five and the park was clearing of people.

The remnants of their picnic circled him. He uncorked the bottle of wine, their second and last, and filled his paper cup. It would be dark in an hour. Then they would have to go. The park guards didn't welcome night people, didn't know how to deal with them.

For the last three weeks, since their first meeting, he had been with Susan almost every day. In the morning he typed his abstracts — outlines of the cases on small white sheets he pasted into his casebooks. Then he went to class. He had lunch, came back to the dorm, worked and then left to find her. Sometimes she was at home. Sometimes he would search for her in the Square, looking into the stores. Later he went back to the law school and, after dinner with Ford, worked until eleven or twelve. Then he went to Susan's, to talk over the day and hold her. Finally, he crept home to sleep.

Time was catching up on him; he only got four or five hours of sleep a night. The wine had gone to his head immediately, taking the edge off the growing coldness. He stretched out, supporting his head on their knapsack, balancing his wine cup on his chest.

He knew he was burning the candle at both ends, and he knew it wasn't like him. He kept waiting for something to check it. But nothing had come. The wine unlocked great waves of exhaustion. It made him yearn for a deep, peaceful sleep. Was it all wasted energy — trying to balance Susan and the law school?

Law. Cases. The endless defining of irrational human actions into tight little patterns. How could he deal with others' actions, when he had absolutely no idea of his own? What sort of pattern was he making as he moved among the great stone buildings of the law school, or along the twisting Cambridge streets with Susan?

Susan gave him no sustenance. When he went to her apartment, or even on the picnic, he went as her guest. I'm going to tell her, he thought, I'm going to tell her that she's going to have to put herself out.

He felt her arm slide over his side; she lay on the ground,

curled against his back. The wind blew her long brown hair over his neck.

"Are you asleep?" she whispered.

"No, I'm thinking. Susan, I haven't done a damn bit of work in a month." He fell asleep. His mind completely gave way, and he rolled over on his stomach, put his arms under his head for a pillow and slept.

When he woke up it was dark and still. He jumped to his feet. His body was shivering, twitching. Around him were dark outlines of trees. For a minute he was lost, and then suddenly he knew. He was still in the park, alone. He looked at his watch and in a while began to see in the dark. It was nine o'clock.

He exploded in anger. The bitch. Jesus. "That's the way it is," he said out loud, and started walking home.

It took him an hour to get back to the dorm. His body was stiff from sleeping on the ground and the walk in the cold. He took off his clothes in the bathroom, got into the shower and let the steam fill up the room. He listened to conversations in the other stalls. It had been an adventure, he told himself, and that was worth something. Now he could get to work. Anyway, he was glad things were settled. He knew he wouldn't call her, not now. He didn't expect her to call — though he knew he'd jump for the next few weeks when the hall phone rang.

He wrapped a towel around himself and walked down the hall to his room smiling. Ford was waiting for him.

"What are you so happy about?" Ford asked. He was sitting on the chair, with his feet on the bed.

Hart pulled Ford up by the arm and started to put a sheet on the bed.

"I've been sleeping in the park. It's great. Try it sometime."

"You missed a meeting of the study group," Ford said.

"So what." The study group was the last thing on Hart's mind. "Anyway, I won't miss any more. I'm through leading a crazy life. I'm going to settle down and work. And I'm going to bed."

He threw the towel on the floor and got under the covers.

"Look, man, I've been sleeping under the stars for three hours, and I feel like hell. Do we have to talk about the study group now?"

Ford smiled at Hart, all tucked into his bed with the covers pulled up to his chin.

"Kingsfield is having a party in two weeks. You got an invitation. I put it on your desk."

"Christ," Hart said, and closed his eyes. "He just won't leave us alone, will he?" He fell immediately to sleep.

Hart woke early. There wasn't any noise: no pages turning quietly, no water running. He pulled on his jeans and a shirt and walked into the hall barefoot. He was a spy and he crept along the corridor, pausing outside the doors, looking for little streams of light that would show someone was still studying.

It was some kind of record. Jesus. The last person still awake, or the first one up. He walked to the door of Ford's room and pushed it slowly open, all the time trying to achieve complete silence, but the door squeaked as it moved.

Ford was there, lying on his back, still dressed, like a Mexican taking a siesta except that Ford's sombrero was a law book spread out over his face, his nose stuck into the binding. It was too early to be serious and Hart started to close the book over Ford's nose. Then Ford was up. He slept lightly and his eyes were glaring as he pivoted on his elbows and leaned toward Hart.

"What the fuck time is it?" Ford said loudly. Hart put his hand down over Ford's mouth and held a finger to his lips. Ford got the idea and tiptoed with Hart to the door. They peeked around the corner and saw that the hall was quiet and empty. Hart hadn't felt so good since summer camp.

Ford turned back to get his shoes, but Hart caught his shoulder, pulled him on and, like cats, they crept outside. There weren't any groundsmen, or police, or students, or birds. There wasn't anything, except the huge stone buildings.

They walked to Langdell because it was the biggest thing they could see and stopped in front of the steps leading up to the main door surrounded by stone carvings. There was no light on in Langdell, except for a spot over the door. They couldn't see the roof. The building stretched up, the top lost in the dark.

"That goddamned building talks to me," Ford said, standing motionless before the steps, staring at the door. "It comforts me, it restores my soul. Even though I walk into it for class, it covers me . . ."

Hart looked at him, and kept looking after Ford finished talking. For a minute he thought that Ford was really crazy, not just peculiar. Ford kept standing at attention, gazing at the library door while the sun began to come up, just the first light.

After a while they walked away. Around the back of Langdell, a small window, in the bottom of a culvert dug next to the wall, attracted Ford. He slid into the pit and nudged the glass. The window swung open. Ford pushed himself through, hung for a second from the sill and then dropped down into the darkness, landing on the cold cement floor. Hart wavered, wondering, and then dropped down too. They both crouched in the dark, letting their eyes adjust.

A putrid wetness lay like soft wax on the tunnel floor. Hart had visions of fungus growing out of green slime, reaching up between his fingers and around his bare toes.

"Light a match," he said.

Though Ford didn't smoke, in college he'd got the habit of carrying matches for other people and so he lit one. It cast a small light, allowing them to see the lockers on either side of the tunnel, but no more than ten feet down the tube into the underbelly of Langdell.

"This is our chance," Hart said. "We can burn the whole school down." Of course, he was wrong. They couldn't burn Langdell down because it was made of concrete and stone. Built to last. The match burned to the end, stung Ford, and he dropped it on the moist floor where it sputtered out.

They inched forward until they were under the library, under the middle of big gray Langdell, down in the heart of the beast, down in its soggy guts.

A stairway led off to the right, up into the stacks. They took it, wanting to climb out of the soft, suffocating slime of the trench. Two floors up, they reached the exact center of the monolith: rows and rows of crumbling manuscripts, rows and rows of smelly Law Reviews. All arranged in tight aisles so that fat men couldn't come down the stacks and get their books. It was quiet, calm. The mass of paper absorbed everything, sucked the noise from the night. And they couldn't see a thing. Not only did the paper kill the noise, it also cut out every bit of light. The rays got confused trying to filter in and out and around the books set in a classic maze.

Hart looked at his watch. The luminous dial worked in

the black void. It was nearly five. Where the hell was Ford? Hart jerked around in the tight row of books and his shoulder jolted a volume. He could feel it teetering on the shelf but couldn't see it. Its fall made a quiet noise, but set in the middle of a noise desert, it seemed like an explosion. He got out Ford's name.

"You stupid asshole," Ford whispered. "I'm right behind you."

They waited, listening to see if their noise would set off other noises. Hart was about to make a crack about being scared of the dark, when he saw the light, just the smallest flicker, coming like a white string out of the dark, leading to the far corner of the stack. It was there, a real light, and it meant that someone else was in the library.

"Ford," Hart whispered, and Ford came up behind him, peering over his shoulder.

"Yes," Ford said, "a light."

They crept along, Ford behind putting his feet into Hart's steps. The passage led into a long narrow corridor from which rows of stacks ran like the teeth of a comb. At the end of the corridor was the source: a glass door far away where the corridor took another turn.

It was irresistible. Finally, they were outside the door. There wasn't any name on it, but they could see the dim outline of a figure inside.

It was getting toward five-thirty. Maybe time to go home. After all, it was against the rules to be in the stacks without a special pass. The stacks weren't for the novice. During the day they were patrolled. Even professors from the college had trouble getting in.

But leaving never occurred to Hart because he knew who the figure was. There wasn't any question. The figure was pacing, moving in a circle. Hart could tell by the gestures — so ingrained in his mind that the smallest movement set off a special blast. His stomach fluttered, contrary instincts swept through him. It wasn't a game anymore. It wasn't fun to be climbing around the stacks. They weren't children.

The walker moved past the translucent glass door, circled again and Ford got nervous. Each circle brought the walker nearer the door. Ford pulled on Hart, drew him into the nearest row of books, far enough to immerse them in darkness.

They heard the door open. Then the light went out and the door closed. They heard footsteps. A shadow passed them, moved steadily away — the steps confident, as if the walker didn't need light, he knew the library so well.

"Kingsfield," Hart said. "I can tell." The words choked him.

On tiptoe, they retraced their route, back into the tunnel and out their window. The dawn had come, laying a sheen of light on Langdell that caught hold in the stone, making it sparkle a faint red and orange, colors they had never thought the stone had.

Far off, on the other side of the yard, the black figure of Kingsfield walked along an asphalt path, alone and carefully. They hugged the side of the library, watching him go. Every now and then he bent down, picked up a piece of litter off the path and put it in his coat pocket. When he stopped, they could make out the chain on his vest, a golden ribbon reflecting the sun that was just clearing the trees behind them.

After Kingsfield had left the parking lot and the sound of the car had died, they walked back to the dorm and became the first students in the breakfast line.

9

KEVIN ANSWERED a question. He just stuck his hand up and answered a question. He had to do it. He didn't think about the answer, or the question, or anything.

He had tried before. He had had the answer all right. He had been as sure of the answer as you can be of anything. But he had hesitated, and then someone else had answered the question and Kevin had sunk down into the chair cursing himself.

He just did it, just answered. He hadn't expected to be called on. He hadn't thought past the moment when he would raise his hand. All he'd really wanted was just the first part: raising the hand and being recognized by Kingsfield.

Now he was stuck because he had answered the question wrong, and Kingsfield had stayed with him, using him as a foil to bring out the truth, to show the rest of the class how "easy" it was to go wrong. Kevin was contributing. But he knew exactly the part he was playing and he was having a harder and harder time talking.

Most of the class was bored, ignoring Kingsfield and Kevin, looking at the portraits or trying to read ahead. Leaving Kingsfield to his private battles. There were only twenty minutes left of class. Leaves were falling outside the tall windows.

"Now, Mr. Brooks, suppose I write a contract. It says: 'I agree for one hundred dollars to paint your car with white paint.' Is there anything different between this contract and one which says: 'You agree to pay me one hundred dollars, provided I paint your car with white paint.'?"

Kevin looked at Kingsfield. What was it Kingsfield had said? He could not hold the hypothetical in his mind. His mind was outside him, looking in. He was watching himself and he couldn't bring it all together, lock into Kingsfield's words.

"I'm not sure I understood it all," Kevin said. "Could you tell me it again?"

"No, Mr. Brooks, but I will tell you this: in the first case we have two mutual promises, the second is a condition on a promise. You know the difference between a condition on a promise and a promise? Will you tell the class?"

Kevin knew the difference. He did his work. But he just couldn't bring it into his conscious mind. He hated himself. But he was unable to focus on the material he had read only the night before.

Hart was watching from his seat to the left of Kevin's. He had witnessed the whole process. Kevin's raising his hand had surprised him. He knew Kevin had never answered a question on his own before. And he knew Kevin was taking it the wrong way. But why had he tried to answer a question? Why had he put himself into this position? Hart wanted to do something to stop it. He had raised his hand, trying to take the burden off Kevin, but he had been ignored. Kingsfield knew a good one when he saw one. Hart wanted to talk to Kingsfield, whisper to him to stop.

Then it was quiet in the big room. The breeze intensified, throwing a brown curtain of leaves against the windows. Hart gave up trying to save Kevin. He felt as if Kevin and Kingsfield were cutout figures against the brown background. Jesus, the wind was exciting. The first cold wind of the year. He wanted to run in it. He wished class would end.

"Yes, I did read the materials before class," Kevin said.

"It just slipped my mind." Kingsfield was standing on the edge of the stage, his hands on his hips, looking severe.

Then Kevin's voice broke. His words no longer came in an even tone. Suddenly the sentences, quiet, long sentences, began to sound like a song, turning up at the ends. The class heard and looked at Kevin. There was some laughter, quiet, suppressed, but audible.

From across the classroom, Hart heard Ford's voice coming out powerfully: "Could you give me the hypothetical over again? I didn't understand it."

It was a shock, hearing the voice without the preparation of a hand, and the class was suddenly back listening.

Kingsfield looked over, trying to identify the speaker. He looked down at the chart to get his name. In that moment, he lost the thread of the problem he was addressing to Kevin.

"Yes, Mr. Ford, do you know the difference between a condition on a promise and a promise?" He said it quickly, wanting to assert himself over the intruder.

10

THE NEW TIE was four inches wide, an inch wider than the ties Hart had brought from Minnesota and a compromise. He had easily rejected the gaudy ties which covered his chest like a vest. But even this one, which was dark and understated, made him slightly uncomfortable. As if with it on, he could only thrust himself forward, could not possibly hide in the corners of the party.

Standing outside Kingsfield's house, with brightly lit porch lights and students going in through the front door, he felt untrue to himself. He should have stuck with his character, and his old ties.

His palms began to sweat again and he thought to himself, out loud in his mind, "Control, control, control." He walked up the steps. The humming of voices like electric typewriters. He opened the door and walked in. A maid popped out of nowhere, took his coat and directed him toward the living room.

At the double door he met a sea of about sixty students, clustered in groups of five, with one group, perhaps twenty people, gathered around a hidden seated figure whom he thought must be Kingsfield.

He caught a drink from a passing tray, maneuvered himself around the groups, avoiding the clutter of furniture — dainty hardwood tables with little silver objects on them holding cigarettes, matches and candies.

Ford's back was to him, but he knew it was Ford. No sport coat, no tie, looking intently at a print on the wall behind a sofa.

"Jesus, if this is supposed to give us closer contact with the faculty, someone has made a terrible mistake," Ford said. "Did you know that Kingsfield has been giving these parties for the last twenty years? He does it for every first year class."

"It makes me nervous," Hart said.

"It shouldn't," Ford replied. "Everyone is getting bombed, or trying to kiss Kingsfield's ass. No one will remember anything. Just imagine that you can vanish or materialize any time you want. Have you said hello to Kingsfield yet?"

"He's over in the corner. It looks too crowded," Hart said, nodding in the direction of the group around the sitting figure.

"No, that's his daughter." Ford smiled. "Can you believe that Kingsfield has a daughter? He's in the study, running this party like he runs the class: fear, and trying to make us feel that we're lucky to be here. He's with his pictures of the Law Review of 1929, his casebooks and a big leather chair. He needs the setting. But I'll tell you something, I like him. He's an asshole, but at least you can grab onto him."

Hart would have been content to stay there, but Ford put his glass into Hart's hand — "You can keep it," he said — and disappeared.

Hart walked to the throng in the corner. The students were thick around her. A couple of very well dressed confident-looking boys dominated the inner circle.

Then Hart felt it. He came into the circle, pushed through the back lines and stopped where he could look down into the chair. It was an electric shock, a sonic boom, the middle of an atomic blast. There in the chair, where Kingsfield's daughter should have been sitting, was Susan, her face riveted on the nearest students. She drew out a cigarette. She smokes, Hart thought: Jesus Christ, she smokes. Twenty lighters clicked. Twenty hands reached down to the cigarette. She lowered her face to the nearest flame and, as she exhaled, looked back over the crowd and saw Hart.

It was a blind disorderly retreat. He stepped back into the crowd, placed his drink on a table and went through the front door without his coat.

"Excuse me," he heard as he stood in the yard. He saw the maid holding his coat. Behind her, coming out of the door, was Susan.

She tried to look serious, but the attempt failed. "Going home?" she asked. "Why, you haven't introduced yourself to my father. Why don't I take you in to meet him?"

He tried to stare with his most piercing, most I-have-great-internal-rage look.

She came down from the steps and took his arm: "I've spent the required hour. Let's walk."

"It's all different now," Hart said. "The way you're dressed." He cursed himself for wearing his new tie.

They were walking in the quietness of the old houses and the trees in the small front yards. The air was heavy, warm, Floridalike air.

"I can't believe that you're mad. On the other hand, I don't know why I'm humoring you." She let go and moved slightly away from him. "Do you think I've fooled you? Or could you be jealous? No, not that. Confused. You must be confused. Tell me about your confusion."

He knew that the relationship between them had shifted. Not only that she was his daughter, but also because she had controlled the situation inside the house.

"I don't know." He tried to say it casually. "It was very mysterious, going for car rides late at night, your apartment. I liked taking you as you were, not putting you against any background. Why didn't you tell me you were Kingsfield's daughter?"

"I didn't want to be put against any background. Anyway, I'm not his daughter very much. I do things like this because he wants me to, but that's all." She took his arm again and she felt it had relaxed.

"Where was your mother?" Hart asked.

"Do you want to know everything about me? Shit, we don't even know each other." He had never heard a girl say shit before.

"Is she dead?" he asked.

"As a matter of fact, she's blown her mind. She's in a mental hospital, crazy as hell." Hart tensed.

"I'm not," she added.

11

SUSAN SAT ALONE on the bed. The green light from the painted bulb kept the room dark and allowed her to see the tops of the houses across the street. She knew the room was a mess, but she didn't have the energy to clean it, not now, so late at night. She would clean it the next afternoon. The long cord on her telephone played like a snake across the room and led under a pillow where the receiver was concealed off the hook.

Perhaps it was the living by herself that made her feel so angry lately, she thought. Maybe it was just part of her character, an echo of her father. Hart would come over for a visit later. She vowed not to give him any shit.

On the table by the bed were letters, thirty or more, carefully piled, in chronological order. The leftovers from last year's love affair. She rolled over and picked them up. Letters written to her when Peter was only a quarter of a mile away. Why did they have to write letters when they saw each other daily in classes? Letters written to her from Europe.

She didn't feel anything for Peter now, except that thinking about him made her laugh. But the summer before she had started college, and through the fall and winter, she had really loved him. She had planned it all out. Marry Peter, wait until he finished law school, move to New York, live there while he worked his way up through clerkship, up to being a partner. Live with him through vacations in the Caribbean, through children. Peter smiling with a tanned face.

Hart, hearing the sound of the record player, knocked loudly. The door was unlocked and the knock pushed it open. He walked in, closed the door and went into Susan's bedroom.

He was tired. He stumbled across the small bedroom and sat down on the floor under the window. The contract law he had been studying was fixed in his mind like a map and he couldn't shake it.

"I've been looking at Peter's letters," she said, pointing at the pile. "I was in love with him last year."

The thought of contracts vanished. "Oh," he said.

"No, I didn't really love him." She propped her head up on her hands.

"Oh," he said, trying to seem indifferent.

"Don't you want to hear about this?" she asked. "Don't you have an interest in the wild exciting life I lead?"

"Look, you're going to tell me anything you want to, and not tell me what you don't want to, so go ahead." He thought this was a pretty forceful statement.

"Well, he was this friend I fell in love with. We were down at Dad's place in the Bahamas and we fell in love. But that's not the part I want to tell you. The point is that he became completely dependent on me. He tried to monopolize me when we got back to school. He kept it up with letters, waiting for me at classes, making sure that he knew where I was all the time. His problem was that he wasn't very smart, do you know what I mean?"

Hart thought he did know. He said yes.

"Anyway, I saw other people and it drove Peter wild. He decided he had to tame me. But as I told you, Peter was stupid. He had an affair to make me jealous. Of course, it freed me. I didn't degenerate completely, sleep with everyone, but I stopped sleeping with Peter, not because of the moral implications, but because he just didn't turn me on anymore."

Hart began to get a tingly feeling.

"Of course, it all made Peter go wild. He quit school and went to Europe. I had completed his transformation. He left in blue jeans, with the beginnings of a beard and a knapsack. On some odyssey to catch some of the things he'd missed out on. It was pathetic watching him go.

"I went to the airport with him, I guess to acknowledge the fact that he was taking a bold step, and to make sure he got on the plane."

She had rolled over on her back, looking up at the ceiling. She had her arms at her sides like a mummy, pressing them into the bed, lifting herself up slightly, doing a casual exercise.

"The letters are funny" . . . 'my dearest . . . what is life without you' . . . Terrible. Peter had a hard time communicating the depth of his feeling. It all started out very seriously and ended as a comedy. I think you can only take your first love affair seriously and then, only if it happens to you when you're young enough to take it to heart. The difference between Peter and me was that I was smart and Peter was stupid. If I hadn't helped him, he'd still be going to law school and raising stupid kids in the suburbs. I banished him to the colonies because I was tougher."

12

"WHAT ARE WE going to do about practice exams?" Kevin asked.

Exams. The word made the study group look up from

their notes. Except Hart. He was gazing out the window, in better shape now because he was getting some sleep, but thinking about other things.

"Nothing," Ford said. "Practice exams don't count. We aren't going to do a thing. Just keep pointing toward the end of the year, Kevin. You'd just have to relearn it all then anyway."

"But we can find out how we stand. You know, whether one of us needs special help," Kevin said.

"You need special help," Bell said. "And you too, O'Connor. You both need shrinks." Bell chuckled to himself.

The beginnings of Bell's property outline were nestled strategically between his arms. Two hundred tattered yellow sheets, wrapped in clear plastic. His eyes kept moving from side to side, and when Hart, sitting next to him, looked over, Bell shielded the papers with a palm. As if Hart were cheating.

"I agree with Ford," Anderson said. "I've given the problem considerable thought and in terms of maximum grade point, the most sensible thing is not to study. Use the exam as a check on your studying habits. See how much you retain as a result of normal studying procedure. Then you will be able to measure accurately how much extra studying you will need for the real test at the end of the year."

Hart saw a sparrow fly down and land on the grassy yard between the dorms. He watched it pecking among some leaves.

"I thought we might all study together for practice exams," Kevin said, looking down at the table. "It would give us a chance to see how we'll work together at the end of the year."

"Listen, Kevin," Ford said, "we don't have time to get up for this exam. It doesn't count."

"What I'd really like to do is talk about the way to take the exam," Kevin said.

"It's not so bad an idea," O'Connor said, pulling himself up so he seemed taller and glaring at Bell. "I'd like a session on examsmanship."

"You need someone to hold your hand?" Bell muttered. The words grated on Hart's ears. His eyes lost their focus on the sparrow.

"Kevin, there isn't enough time," Ford said. "Listen, they don't count. Listen to Anderson, he knows what he's talking about."

Ford shuffled his notes together and looked away from Kevin. "All right," Ford said, clearing his throat, "I want to get into the statute of frauds today . . ."

Kevin cut him off. "I'm not ready yet." He spat out the words and then was surprised and unsure.

Ford swung his head over to Kevin slowly, looked him up and down. He tapped his pencil down on the table.

"The whole statute is given on page fifteen hundred," Ford said. "We'd better go over it together, before we review what was said in class."

Kevin's face went red and then drained of color. He half rose from the table.

"Who do you think you are? King shit? You don't run things. You don't run me," Kevin yelled.

Hart put his hands up to his head, covering his ears with his fingers and his eyes with his palms. But he could still hear Ford's answer, coming in a quiet monotone.

"You talk too much, Kevin, and you give everyone around here a pain in the ass. If you don't like things, leave. But figure on this. We can get along without your outline. Can you get along without ours?"

50

Hart stood up. He felt sick. He put his hands down on the table and bent over so his head was only a foot from Ford's.

"Shut up, will you," Hart hissed. "Just shut up."

When I was an undergraduate we cornered McNamara in the street. About two thousand of us surrounded him and lay down in the road, not letting him leave.

Finally, he agreed to answer three questions and climbed on top of a car. A skinny boy with glasses was standing near the car. He screamed in McNamara's face: "How many children have been killed in Vietnam?"

McNamara said the question was unfair: no one had any idea how many.

The boy tensed into a steel rod, his face turned red, his body bent forward. With all the power he had he screamed back: "Why don't you know, don't you CARE?"

13

Hart was standing in Kingsfield's study. He hadn't been able to sleep and, leaving Susan in the large bed upstairs, had come down and wandered through the house until he found the small study, perched behind the living room.

He had turned on only the desk lamp. He wasn't quite sure that the neighbors, knowing that Professor Kingsfield was gone for the weekend, would assume that it was Susan in the house.

The desk was surprisingly small. The same clutter of objects that filled the other rooms but more personal — an engraved ashtray and pen set. The pictures on the wall fascinated him most. A picture of Susan, about five years old, standing on the beach smiling. She looked different in short curly hair. A picture of the three of them together; Kingsfield, Susan, and her mother, a pretty woman, smiling, holding the hands of the other two.

"Are you interested in the study?" Susan had crept up on him in the dark, following the study light. It startled him, having her there without warning. Sleeping in her father's bed was one thing but he felt like an intruder in the study. She picked up an oblong inscribed silver box, opened it and produced a cigar. Brushing by Hart, she sat behind the desk and struck a match on the big leather chair.

"I played in this study when I was a little girl. I used to run the Dictaphone." She leaned back in the chair, striking the pose of the Columbia student who had been photographed in Grayson Kirk's office. The allusion was lost on Hart. But the sight of her naked, smoking her father's cigar and leaning back in the chair made him nervous. She could do it — it was her father — but he was an intruder.

"Sit down, boy," she said, in mock seriousness. "They tell me you have special problems. Maybe you ought to get involved with a nice girl and settle down."

She opened the cabinet behind the desk, took out a bottle of bourbon and poured Hart a glass. "Have a drink of this, son, it will give you strength for the battle ahead."

He sat down with the drink.

Behind Susan's head was a graduation picture of thirty or so serious, suited young men. Kingsfield was in the middle of the group. Susan could tell Hart was looking past her.

"That's the Law Review of 1929: two chief justices, and Dad. He put the picture where you have to look at it."

"I feel funny," Hart said. "This is his special room." He picked up the silver ashtray. It had an inscription on it, a squash prize, 1926. "Do you think he'd like us drinking in his room?"

"Hell," Susan said. "He's in New York. He'll never know you or I were here. There is absolutely nothing, nothing, not one thing in the entire world, to worry you. You just lean back and talk to me. Besides, don't you think he'd want you to see it all? You're behaving just the way he'd want you to behave. Picking up his little silver mementos, looking at his Law Review picture. You act like a student in a seminary. It's just what he'd want. To have you fondle his things."

She blew the smoke out of her mouth in a hard push and looked at Hart as though she was tired. He smiled, trying to break her new mood. He put his feet up on the desk, touching her toes with his.

"You know, Susan, when I'm in class with your father I feel like he knows me, as though when he calls on me he had it all planned out, like he's watching my progress. I feel like we're talking about things. You know, when he asks me a question, like he cares about how I do."

She turned in her chair, looked past him, took a sip of her drink and laid the cigar on the table. Then she looked directly at his eyes, hard. She took a deep breath.

"You're going to get screwed. You're a nice guy but you're going to get screwed. There isn't any middle ground. If you start thinking like that you'll never be able to survive. Hell, it's all got to roll off your back. Do you think my father even knows who you are? Do you think he'd care, even if he did know? What do you think law school is all about? You have to ignore it, or you have to be able to take it. You have to float with it or you have to wade through not thinking it's there."

Hart was surprised she'd taken it so seriously. He put the little ashtray back on the table. "Listen," he said, "you're a beautiful naked girl sitting right across from me and if you start getting serious, you'll blow my mind."

He got up and came around the desk, put a hand around her head and pulled it into his chest. He stood that way, waiting for her to move.

14

HART GOT BACK to the dorm late Sunday night. He dropped his books on the bed and then turned on the light. Standing by the window, dressed in his vest and suit pants with a striped tie fluffed neatly away from his white shirt, was Toombs.

"Oh, hello," Toombs said.

"Can I do something for you?" Hart said, angry to be back

in the dorm and angry that someone had come in without asking.

"Can I do something for *you?*" Toombs said. "I finished working and I thought you might like to talk about your dorm problems."

"No," Hart said, "I don't want to talk about my dorm problems. I don't want to talk to anyone."

Toombs walked to the door.

"Remember that I'm always here. I want you to ask me things. I want you to feel you can rely on me."

Hart nodded and turned away. He stayed that way, not looking at the door and not moving until, five minutes later, he heard Toombs walking away down the hall. Then Hart went to Ford's room.

He'd tried to catch Ford Saturday afternoon, after the study group meeting. Ford had been out, maybe trying to avoid him. He hadn't meant to scream at Ford.

The room was empty. Hart sat down on the bed to wait. He thought about Toombs, and somehow the thought made him feel he'd sit there and wait for Ford until morning if it took that long. On the desk he saw Ford's journal. He bent over, not really figuring on reading it, but not avoiding it either. He'd hear anyone walking down the hall because the door was half open.

. . . had dream last night. Boy in black pants, white shirt, stole my tennis racket. I went down to my car (VW bus) and in it was a Negro boy, very young, and two policemen.

All four of us went after the thief. The car (bus) had been in the city, but was now in the country — we saw the thief running ahead. I jumped out of the car and ran after the thief, and so did the police and the Negro boy. The thief got away.

Then the Negro boy took a gun and started firing at the

police and me. I ducked, and the policeman started firing back.

Then one of the policemen turned so his back was to the boy. He threw his gun over his shoulder in a high lob. It landed in the boy's hand. Now he had two guns . . . I started inching away.

There were noises in the hall. Hart stopped reading. He felt very tired and went back to his room to sleep.

15

SUSAN STOOD at the window in her bedroom, looking out over the roofs of Cambridge. Hart's hands were around her. There was no light on in the room, so they could spy out without being seen.

The softness of the wind. It crept through her hair around Hart's face. Hart felt as if he was in the time just before sleep, when you think very hard to know where you are.

"What are we going to do in the summer?" he whispered. He wanted to say, I love you.

"I don't know," Susan said, "we'll just wait and find out." She put her hands on his, pulling his arms around her.

"If we don't think about it now, it won't just happen. I'll go to Minnesota, you'll stay here," he said. He wanted to say, I love you. Everything is all right. Yes, dearest, we'll always be together.

She turned around, put her arms around his waist, looked into his face. He felt like a statue and he looked out the window, over her head, conscious that she was watching him.

"People get married when there are wars," she said, "because they're scared and want some calm. I don't know, maybe they do it because they want to feel they have too much at stake for God to hurt them."

She left him and went into the living room. He lay down on the bed, staring up at the ceiling. He felt hurt and he wanted to feel hurt. There was some dignity in that. He wanted to do something. Maybe to grab her and tell her that she was going to marry him and that was that and she could just learn to live with it. Sweep her off her feet. Or maybe put his head down and walk quietly past her out the door without saying anything, not turning when she asked where he was going. Two sides of the same coin. He just didn't know what the hell to do because he couldn't guess anything about what she would do.

"I don't know what to do about you," he called into the next room. "I never know what you want."

She came in and sat on the bed, looking down at him.

Her brown hair came close together in the front, hiding her face, making her look soft and cuddly, like a teddy bear. She was so tiny, he thought. He looked into her face and he felt that she was small and delicate. The only light came from the window and it dissolved her face into her hair, making it hard to see the outlines.

"Listen, Susan, I really want to talk to you. You know, really say things to you. I don't want to fake it." Why, he thought, why should I be with her, if I can't talk to her? Why is it her and not someone else?

She tucked her legs under her and leaned across the bed so her back rested against the wall.

"This room's no good. I want a rug. You can't have the bed right down on the floor when there isn't any rug. I get splinters sometimes." She drew the blanket, piled on the end of the bed, up around her.

"There isn't anything in this room," she said quietly. "Just

58

the bed and the window, nothing else. The only decoration is the green light bulb. I used to think that was the only way to appreciate a room for what it is, to have nothing in it so you could see the walls and floor and everything. Now I want to put some things in it, but I don't know what kind of furniture to get. I don't know what I want."

Hart looked over at the window, at the floor, at the walls. There wasn't anything else in the room, except the bed, put right down on the floor.

"You always talk to me in riddles," he said. "Listen, don't you know what I want? Don't you know what I mean? I want to get away from all the shit we give each other. I want to really talk. I want to tell you how I really feel about you. I don't want to plot about it. I don't want to do things, thinking about what you're going to do.

"I want to cut out all that middle stuff. I want us to be like one nerve. I want to tell you the truth and then have you tell me what you really think about it. I want it to be quick, like a game. I want us to react."

"All right," she said. "React." She pulled the blanket tight around her. She looked down at him and he looked away at the wall.

"Shit," he said. "I was ruined by my childhood."

He laughed, first to himself, then out loud, just a little, and smiled. "The only kind of girls I'll ever get to know are ones who go on dates. I'll have to go to a dating bar. I just don't know how to talk. I don't have any objective. I'm not trying to make it with you. I can't try to impress you. I don't have any dreams, or hopes, or plans. I just don't have any plans."

He stretched his arms out and pulled her down next to him. She let herself fall and put her head on his chest.

"Am I worthless?" he said.

"What would you like to happen?" Susan said.

"I suppose we could get married, or we could stop seeing each other, or just go on the way we are now."

"Your problem is that you don't like not knowing what you want. Why do you have to want anything? Don't do anything. If anything happens to make it seem like the insides of us want each other, then it'll work out. Let's not let outside things push us together or apart. I don't want you now, but I'm interested in finding out how it will come out."

WINTER

16

HART AND FORD, their feet up on the windowsill, drinks in their hands, watched the snowflakes dart in and out of the light like fish in an aquarium. This wasn't the first storm. It snowed every few days, covering all the cars and for a few hours leaving everything neat. The snow would stop, get a ragged, used look to it. Slushy, uneven, brown. The streets would turn to sewers and wait for a rain to wash it all out.

"The trouble with going to sleep here is that there are no surprises. You know what I mean? There are surprises in the summer," Ford said.

"No," Hart said, "I don't know."

"Last summer," Ford said," I was lying in bed, six in the morning, sleeping soundly. I always sleep that way at home. I relapse and let the warmth ooze around me. I was sleeping and suddenly I felt this soft thing shaking around in the bed."

"A rat, a snake. Maybe a turtle?"

"No." Ford chuckled to himself. "One of my sister's friends. I think she was fourteen. She'd been reading all kinds of stuff. So she snuck over and lay down in bed with me. Nude. Scared the hell out of me. Statutory rape. Twenty years. I kicked her out."

Hart looked away from the window. He swirled the ice in his glass.

"It's not funny," he said. "It's not funny for a fourteen-year-old to jump into bed with you. It's sad."

"I'm not making myself into a folk hero. It's a story. It happened. For Christ's sake," Ford drawled.

"It shouldn't happen," Hart said. "Someone should have

sent her to a shrink. It's pathetic. It's sick. Shit, Ford."

Ford thought for a while.

"Midwesterners are archaic," he said finally. "Like animals. You're always on the hall phone, calling your girl friends. Don't you see how screwed up that is? Call your girl friends? Everything in the world is happening, while you're sitting around reading cases or calling your girl friends."

"I don't know," Hart whispered. "I really don't know what the fuck is going on. I don't understand anything."

"You're too late," Ford said. "Understanding things was what college was for. What did you do in college? We spent hours on it. Dissecting sex, virginity, love, fucking in general. I had a roommate like you. One night he found out his girl in Kansas had been sleeping with, hell, maybe three or four people. I spent hours with him, walking him around the Square."

"I believe it," Hart sighed, the words hanging in the air.

"You know, right now," Ford said, "or tomorrow, when you're thinking about contracts, forty thousand teen-agers are jumping into bed with each other. Forty thousand teen-agers are getting pregnant, killing themselves. Fucked up, crazy-ass kids. Everything is happening."

Hart put his drink on the sill, put his elbows on his knees, his head in his hands.

"God, I'm sick of it," Hart moaned. "Jesus Christ."

"I'm sick of it too," Ford said, leaning over so his mouth was right by Hart's ear. "I'm sick of all the theories. I give a shit if some chick in Kansas loses her virginity. There's only one sensible thing to do in this mess. Find a good woman and hang on. Hang on like hell. I mean, throw yourself into the goddamned struggle like a maniac. Grab onto her boobs and don't let go."

17

KEVIN AIMED the repeater out the window, sighting down the street. It was six in the morning and the street was empty. Every five or ten minutes, a car or a dog would come by.

His room was filled with his notes and law books, laid randomly on the sofa, coffee table and chairs. He'd spent the night trying to catch up.

A Volkswagen turned the corner, puttering up the street, right under the window, moving slowly because of the ice. He leaned out, aiming at the middle of the engine cover, between the air ducts, focusing on the castle symbol. He squinted and pulled the trigger.

The gun went *ping* as the hammer fell on the empty chamber. It was bad to pull the trigger when there wasn't anything in the gun, but he didn't like it anyway. It was a present from Asheley's father.

He felt almost tired enough to go to bed.

18

THEY WERE on the top of a hill. Out the windshield, Hart could see a long thin expanse of snow and down below it he knew there must be ice. The lake curved around to the left, behind far trees. A large brick building towered beside them. Susan let the motor idle.

"The museum isn't open. We got here too late," she said.

"Listen, let's at least talk about things," he said. "We've got to get organized."

"Christ," she said, low and under her breath.

"I'm sorry. Really, I'm sorry."

"Why? You feel it," she answered. "Why not say what you feel?"

"We could get married and *then* live together."

"Jesus, I told you, I don't mind sin. I just *want* to live alone."

"It would work," he said.

She shut off the engine and the heater stopped with it.

"I don't have anything else to say. I don't want to live in the married student dorms, have neat friends down the hall and walk babies with them. They put people away in that place. And I don't want to live with you. Organize yourself some other way."

He got out and slammed the door; stood watching the lake.

They ran down the hill, making wide tracks in the snow, finally reached the lake and started to walk around it, keeping to the ice at the sides. He wished he'd worn boots, or at least something with rubber soles.

"Hart," she said at last, "there are things I'm trying to do."

"What?"

"Live alone," she said.

When he kicked down, he thought he could feel the ice respond, quiver to the touch.

"How deep is the lake?" he asked.

"Deep."

"All right, I said I was sorry. Everything is coming unstuck. I just can't play anymore."

"I wasn't ever playing," she said.

They veered away from the shore. He worried because he didn't know the lake and couldn't see the color of the ice.

"I don't understand it," she said. "How I get mixed up with law students. It's some curse that follows me around.

Something my father must arrange. You haven't seen him lately?"

"Just in class . . ."

"You're all crazy . . . all the law students. You can't let things alone. Hart, something is happening to your mind."

He walked straight out from the shore. You should stay apart on the ice so that, if it gives way, you can get to each other. You crawl out on your belly. He'd learned that in Boy Scouts. He put his arm around her, loosely, as if they were old friends.

"You've got to understand that I'm real," she said, "that I'm going to live past twenty. You've got to put your head in mine."

They were almost to the center, one hundred yards from shore.

"I can't," he moaned, "I can't. I don't know why things are good, and I don't know why they are bad."

The ice cracked.

It sounded like it came from a long way off, a wave far out, reaching in to them. He could feel it move beneath them, lift his feet up and then down, slowly, like a slow motion picture of a trampoline. He fell over, turning in the air, landing with his arms stretched out, spread-eagled on the ice.

"Christ," she said. "Christ, this will kill us."

She was still standing, her arms outstretched like a tightrope walker, balancing herself.

The water seeped over his hands. His breathing pounded in and out as if it was moving the ice. He welcomed the numbness the water brought. He didn't want to move. He could feel the ice rising and lowering gently beneath him, as if he were lying on an air mattress, a perfect balance. He exhaled ever so lightly and the ice shifted.

"Don't move," she said softly. She started down, like a ballerina coming down for applause. He watched her, as if dreaming. He felt the ice vibrate as she came down.

His hands began to burn, even though they were wrapped in snow. They passed through numbness, out on the other side into heat. So hot he felt they could burn through the ice.

Then she was down, her feet and hands forming four points. The ice breathed. It relaxed, coming up, as she shifted her weight out. She lay, arms outstretched, on her back. He thought what they must look like from the top: like children playing in the snow, making angels.

She started inching, pushed herself with her heels to see if she could and then stopped.

"Go ahead," he said, "get off, and I'll come afterward. Get the fuck out of here."

Am I saying that, he thought.

She pushed, sliding away toward the shore, inching like a worm. The water rose slowly, over his legs, into his pants. Then she was on the shore standing, a speck, waving her arms.

The water covered his hands. His breathing pounded against the cold, moving the ice, but his mind was still. He couldn't even think of moving. His mind had disconnected from his body.

For some insane reason, he thought about cases in contracts, and his mind began to distinguish the cases, make subtle differentiations he'd never been able to do in class.

"Now, slide off, now, now, now . . ." Her voice came from a long way off, echoed across the lake and then came back from the other side.

He tried pushing with the toes of his shoes. The leather squeaked on the ice. It wouldn't push him. He dug in harder and the ice vibrated again. The water came up higher and he heard cracking, popping like firecrackers.

He came back to the lake: woke as if someone had jabbed him with a hot coal.

"Get up. Come off before it caves . . ."

He slid his hands and feet together, slowly, while the ice sank lower: got up like a dog, keeping on four points, and started moving. The ice popped around him, sank but held. Somehow he was fifty yards from shore and then it sank more, and he stood up and ran, sliding his feet over it, not coming down with a bounce.

It popped behind him, as if he were setting off charges with each step. He felt it cave five yards from the shore, and as it gave way — not going down, but floating out to the sides — he gave a push off, sailed out toward the shore as far as he could.

He froze. As soon as the water covered him, the heat in his body left. It paralyzed him from the first second. He tried to touch bottom and he couldn't. He pushed forward in a huge frog kick, slow and clumsy because of the shoes, glided in, and she was around him, up to her waist in the water, pulling him by the shirt.

"You crazy bastard. You crazy . . ." she screamed, her mouth so cold that the words came out choked and high.

"Goddamn, goddamn . . ."

They collapsed on the shore, lying on top of each other in a soggy pile, like wet branches.

She stopped the car in the middle of the street, next to the law school dorms. He put his hand down on the door handle and hesitated.

"It isn't good," she said. "Something's happened to your mind. I thought it might be me, but it isn't. It's you, your mind. I don't think we should see each other for a while. That's the usual thing to do, take time to think about things. You were fresh before, you weren't like other people in Cambridge."

He heard a car idling behind them, wondered how long until its driver would honk.

"I've got to go back and get warm," she said. "I know there are lots of things to say, but it's not worthwhile saying them."

He opened the door, got out and shut it, stood, looking in the car window.

"Think about me," she said, and shifted into first. "And think about yourself. But don't call. You'll want to, but don't."

The car behind honked and he cursed it. She revved the motor, the wheels spun on the ice, gained traction and then the car accelerated, racing down the street, away from him.

19

"You the only one here?" Ford said, skating across the linoleum floor. "I'll go call them." Hart watched Ford shake the snow off his coat.

"Don't bother," Hart said. "It doesn't make any difference. They'll come."

"You're kind of strung out, aren't you?" Ford said, sitting down next to Hart. "What's up?"

O'Connor, Bell and Anderson came in together as Ford spoke. Hart took advantage of the noise and ignored Ford's question.

O'Connor curled into his chair, sitting Indian style to give himself extra height. Bell waited and then took the seat farthest away from him.

Anderson heaved his attaché case and as it gathered momentum on the back swing gave it an extra push up so that it swung neatly, clearing the rim of the table and landing with a dull thud. He put his hands down on either side of the case, shook them like a magician about to do a trick, and sprung the locks. The top popped up: the thirty separate files disengaged and hung between the bottom and lid of the case.

"Material — for — discussion — today?" Anderson said.

"Civil procedure, it's my turn," O'Connor snapped. Anderson slid out the appropriate file and shut his attaché case.

"I tried to call you and let you know I'd be late," O'Connor went on, looking at Ford. "I didn't feel well this morning."

Across the table, Bell was unwinding the plastic cover from his huge property outline even though they weren't going to be discussing property. Under the crinkled plastic were four hundred tattered, yellow sheets. Bell didn't type, and the outline was printed in a neat blue pen. He spent hours on it in the library, drawing each letter like a separate picture.

"Before we get down to business," O'Connor said, "I have a suggestion." He paused to give his words drama, though everyone knew what was coming.

"If it's about organizing the group, I think we should wait until everyone is here," Ford said. "Kevin has an appointment and he's not coming today."

"Come on," O'Connor squeaked, "what difference does Kevin make?"

Bell groaned.

"Please listen," O'Connor said. "None of us has time to meet twice a week. The casebooks have grown like tapeworms. We simply have to get organized. I propose we shift to bi-monthly meetings."

71

"That's crazy," Bell said.

"No, it's not crazy," O'Connor went on. "Our only real gain is sharing outlines at the end of the year, not these asinine talks."

"I want to see you twice a week so that I know you're going to have an outline," Bell said, looking down at the yellow pulp in front of him. "And your outline better be good."

"If you were properly organized, you wouldn't have to worry about the two hours you spend here," Anderson said, raising his eyebrows. "If you regulated yourself, you wouldn't have this problem."

Hart noticed that the snow was beginning to clear.

Ford looked down, leaning over the table.

"It's getting to be half an hour we've wasted," Ford said. "We've had this group from the beginning. It's good luck. Let's get started."

"I'm willing to discuss my course anytime," O'Connor whined. "But I think you should at least give me a fair hearing." His voice trailed off in indignation.

"You're full of it," Bell mumbled. His eyes were bloodshot.

"I don't have time for the group," O'Connor pleaded.

"Regulate yourself, O'Connor," Anderson said.

"Let's start," Ford said.

"No, let's not start." O'Connor's words seemed to choke him. "And I'm tired of you telling me what to do. You aren't even paying attention to my idea."

"O'Connor," Ford lashed out, "at the end of the year, when they're passing out exams and you're trying to stretch high enough to reach the table, you'll regret you deserted this group."

Ford pulled his arms into his body and sat back. His hand brushed Bell's outline.

"Watch it," Bell said.

"I want a vote," O'Connor mumbled. "I want at least a vote."

"I vote we forget your stupid idea," Bell said. Hart, Ford and Anderson raised their hands.

O'Connor looked down, started turning the pages of his civil procedure outline. "All right," he said, "it's just an idea. Do you remember *Pennoyer* versus *Neff?*"

20

KEVIN DIDN'T LIKE to walk down the connecting passages under the law school buildings. Long cement passages, lined with brightly colored lockers, filled with students going to classes. Passages which were always a little damp.

There was nothing to look at. The passages focused his vision straight ahead and he couldn't help meeting the eyes of the people he passed. In high school, he had loved the corridors. Liked the contact with people, saying hello. He just didn't know enough people here and when he said hello to someone he didn't know, he got no response, except a puzzled look.

He took a branching corridor deep beneath the library. There were fewer students in this tunnel and the lockers gave way to translucent glass doors of offices. This tunnel was shabby, lights out every few feet and no light coming through the dirty glass. He stumbled along looking at the name on each office.

He took another turn, darker still. The tunnel walls seemed to close in on him. Then there was a light on in one of the offices. In little black letters the door read: MR. SHAW. Kevin ran his hand over his hair, making sure it was in place, gathered his books together and knocked.

A voice called him in. The office was a little cell, about the size of a dorm room. There were slits of windows high up on the wall and a light bulb without any shade hanging from the ceiling. On the wall above a small bookcase were Mr. Shaw's degrees.

Mr. Shaw motioned Kevin to sit and Kevin sat on the only other chair in the office: it was wooden, high and very old. It swayed slightly when Kevin moved.

"Let's see, you're . . ." Mr. Shaw mumbled.

"I'm Kevin Brooks," Kevin said, remembering to smile.

Kevin was surprised Mr. Shaw was so young. He had thick glasses, curly black unmanageable hair and spoke with a clipped New York accent.

"Oh yes, Mr. Brooks," Mr. Shaw said, rummaging through the papers piled on the top of his little desk.

"I've got to get some light in here. This place was set for renovation, except once they gave it to the graduate students, they forgot about that. Yes, you see, I had this paper, but I just put it down, and now, ho, here it is . . . Yes, Mr. Brooks."

Kevin leaned forward and then swayed backward and forward again on his rockinghorse chair. He was curious. A little scared and curious. Why had Mr. Shaw called him?

"Well, Kevin," Mr. Shaw said, "we've got the results of your practice exams in and I wanted to talk with you about them."

Kevin jerked back in excitement and his chair bobbed back and forth. He put his feet solidly on either side of the legs to brace it, but that only made his bottom the apex of a triangle and the chair vibrated violently. He wanted to hear how he did; he thought he might have done well.

"Well, Kevin," Mr. Shaw said, "I don't know exactly how to put this, but your performance was unusual. No use beating around the bush. You flunked every one of your practice exams."

Jesus, Kevin thought, that can't be true. His chair rocked violently, almost spinning him to the ground. Shit, he thought, why can't they get any decent equipment in this fucking school.

"I'm sorry to be blunt," Mr. Shaw said. "After all, there isn't anything to worry about. As you know, these exams don't count. By the way, if you'll just sit still you won't break my chair. If it goes, I'll never get another one down here. I'm lucky to have this desk. You know that chair is the property of Harvard University."

Mr. Shaw got up from behind his desk and was about to pace, when he realized there wasn't enough room.

"Kevin, I think that we are going to have to give you some special help. We do this from time to time. We have helped a great number of students who started off on the wrong foot."

He couldn't have flunked; they didn't admit law students who would flunk.

"Now, I think we'll have to get to work on this right away, lose no time, you know, because we have to bear in mind that exam time will be on us in almost four months. We want to be prepared.

"What we'll do is this. We have a special program of tutoring by the best of our third year students — don't worry, the law school pays for it. I'm going to assign you to one of them and he'll take it from there. Any questions? Good. Well, then, you take this phone number; call the number and find out when you can meet with your tutor.

Come back in about three weeks and let me know how it's going."

Mr. Shaw opened the door. "Thank you for coming, Kevin."

21

HART PUSHED BACK his chair and stretched, shaking free of six hours in the library. He walked out into the center aisle, between the tables, all manned, and past the humming Xerox machine and the press of students around the card catalogue. Turning left, he followed the Law Reviews — different colors for different schools — as they wound, six shelves high, along the side of the library. When the Law Reviews ended, he followed the State Reporters — Alabama, Alaska, sets of books containing every case heard in the courts of every state. The rows of books looked like railroad tracks nailed to the sides of the library, the only festive addition.

Then they ended and he was in front of glass doors that said: TREASURE ROOM.

He made this circle every few hours and he always stopped at the Treasure Room. He watched the woman at the librarian's desk, sitting alone, circled by empty tables, oak paneling, and bookcases fronted with glass.

On impulse Hart went in. As the doors swung shut, all the scratching pens, the turning pages and the sliding of books stopped. The room was absolutely quiet. And the air: it was cool, moist, so heavy he could taste it.

The woman got up from her table and walked over to him.

"May I assist you?" she said. She wants me to leave, Hart thought; she wants to throw me out of Paradise.

"The air," Hart said, "it's so moist."

"We keep it constant," the woman said. "At the best level to protect the books."

"This would be a fantastic place to study," Hart said. "It doesn't stink, like the library, and there isn't any noise."

He'd said the right thing — she nodded, appreciating his approval of her room.

"Something special must happen here," Hart said.

"This isn't for studying, unless you need one of our important books. This room contains all the famous books — first editions of casebooks, going back to before the Revolution. And, of course, the Red Set."

Just the words, Red Set. The way she said it, kind of moving back from the words and letting them hang out there on their own. He knew he was onto something big.

"The Red Set?" Hart said.

"Yes, the notebooks, the memoranda, first drafts of all the professors' writings. We have them all here. We guard them; keep them."

He walked past her into the middle of the room, and she raced after him.

"This room isn't for studying," she said. "This room isn't for you."

"You mean, you have the original notes of Professor Kingsfield?" Hart said, looking into the glass bookcases, looking for the red bindings. "You say that you have all his words, his notes, everything, in this room?"

"They're not for you," she said.

But he didn't hear her. She was insignificant.

"I want to see Professor Kingsfield's notes on contracts,"

Hart said, staring down at her, snapping out the order.

"I'm afraid we couldn't allow that," she said.

"I must see them," Hart ordered. He drew himself up over her and peered down.

"No," she said. "Absolutely not. It's out of the question, unless you have special authorization. Unless you have Professor Kingsfield's approval."

He backed down. Her eyes were burning and he knew he'd never be able to reason with her.

"Listen," Hart said, "I've found something. Where have you been?"

"I went to the Square to eat," Ford said, collapsing on the bed.

Hart stood over him, his face glowing.

"Did you know they've got a room in the law school that has the professors' notes? I mean the actual notes they took when they were students. They're just sitting there, waiting."

"What were they like?" Ford said.

And then he saw Hart's eyes, big and round, blazing against the blackness outside the window.

"No," Ford said. "Absolutely not. We'd be thrown out of school. Listen, notes are notes. Just paper. Don't kid yourself. They'd be just like ours. They aren't anything."

"The room is called the Treasure Room," Hart said. "The books are called the Red Set."

"Come on," Ford said. "Treasure Room?"

"Really, it's there, all of it, everything."

Ford groaned.

"I'll tell you what," he said after a while. "If I ever really get to hate this place, maybe."

22

"AND FOR FURTHER REFERENCE, you might glance at the
Stubble Rock case," Kingsfield said and then sprang to his
left and asked O'Connor to recite the facts of *Taylor* v.
Cunningham.

"Which case, which case . . ." O'Connor moaned, looking through his book. O'Connor had been called on the day
before. It was unusual to be called on twice in succession
and he had been caught off guard.

Hart thought about Kingsfield's passing allusion to *Stubble Rock*. He was the only student in class who would know
that the obscure *Stubble Rock* case was about a house built
over an old mine, that the foundation had given way, converting the house into a bomb shelter, three hundred feet
below ground, which might have been all right, had not a
mother and three children been killed in the process.

"Oh, *Taylor* versus *Cunningham*," O'Connor said, "the
case on page one thousand three. Right, I read that case."

"Yes, that case and be quick about it," Kingsfield snapped.
"There's a lot to cover today."

Hart knew about *Stubble Rock* because he'd read Kingsfield's article "The Blessings of Consideration," published
thirty years before. He'd looked up all Kingsfield's articles
and read them.

Thirty cases later, class ended. The people in the back
of the room started out, some happy because Kingsfield had
been in particularly good form and others sad because he
hadn't fallen from the podium. Hart got his materials together and looked for Ford.

As Hart watched, Ford's notebook was knocked off the

desk by a student with red hair, pushing to get into the aisle.

"Shit," Ford said, and bent to pick up the pages that had worked loose and were lying in the dirty space under the seats.

"I knew about the *Stubble Rock* case," Hart said absent-mindedly. "It's in an article Kingsfield wrote, 'The Blessings of Consideration.' "

"So what," Ford said. A boy in the next aisle stepped on one of Ford's pages, leaving a black footprint of dirty snow.

"It's just kind of wild," Hart said. "It's cool. I can really understand what he's saying. Most of the people in this class don't have any idea about *Stubble Rock*. I do; Kingsfield does. Don't you see?"

"No," Ford said. He was down on his knees now, under the bench top, getting the last pages.

"Man, my mind is really in his," Hart said. "I know what he's saying before he says it."

"You're sick," Ford said angrily, standing up holding two crinkled pages. "Get your head together. The only important thing is getting out of this place in one piece. You're getting as bad as the guys at lunch who tell stories about him. I mean, those guys are really sad. They're in their second and third year, and instead of doing something healthy — fucking or something — they sit around and re-run what a terrible time they had in contracts. All they can talk about is Kingsfield."

The classroom was almost empty. Outside, they could hear students coming up the stairs from the tunnels. In a minute, the room would be jammed. Ford shoved his papers into the notebook and started for the aisle.

"Don't get pissed off," Hart said, following him. "Do you

think I'm trying to build myself up? Do you think I told you that because I wanted to impress you?"

"Forget it," Ford said. They came to the door, and pushed out into the hall. "Let's walk outside; the tunnels are crowded. I just mean, be yourself, all right? I get enough of Kingsfield in class."

23

STALE CIGAR SMOKE filtered out the door, into the hall. Hart, standing by the dorm telephone, watched it float to the ceiling. He walked to the door and peeked. The bed was turned on its side against the wall. Five students were sitting in a circle, playing poker, communicating by hand signals. They'd been playing all winter.

He started back to the phone, past a door painted black in violation of dorm regulations. The student inside collected towels. He put them under the rug, taped them to the walls. "Soundproofing," he said, and kept to himself. Everyone said he was going to make Law Review but Hart had never seen him in class.

Hart paused, then released the last digit of Susan's number. The dial swung back, the phone connected, started to ring. He didn't have anything to say; he shouldn't be making the call; he hadn't even thought about it . . .

"Hello," Susan said.

"Susan, can I talk to you? Are you busy?" He could hear a record in the background. Were there voices?

"Susan?"

"I told you not to call."

"Listen . . ."

The line went dead. "Good-bye," Hart said into the deaf

receiver and hung up. He went back to his room and lay down on his bed, waiting for his energy to rebuild. Finally, he sat up to unbutton his shirt. The movement revealed his watch: two minutes to twelve. He turned off the light and went to the window.

In two minutes a shriek rattled the glass:

"AHHHHHHHHHHHHHHHHHHHHH . . . EEEEEEE-EEEEEE . . . AHHH . . ."

He pressed his face against the pane, trying to spot the Screamer, the mad law student who screamed every Sunday and Friday night at exactly twelve. The first time, Hart had run out in the hall with the rest of the dorm but now he took it for granted.

Maybe the guy uses amplification, Hart thought.

He gave up watching. There was no sign of a shadow behind any of the dark windows, and in the lighted ones students were looking out through their own reflections.

Halfway to Ford's room, Hart saw a new addition to the hall: a poster of a nude teen-ager lying in a flower bed. He flicked the picture from the door. The paper glided into the middle of the hall and floated to the floor, landing face down. In two days tracked-in grit and snow would eradicate it.

Ford's room was empty. Hart looked twice, because there wasn't a single other person in the dorm he could really talk with. He ate dinner with an assortment of students, said hi to a lot in the hall, but a real talk, lasting into the dawn, was different.

The sheets of Ford's bed were pulled off, crumpled and dirty. Above the desk, Ford's Sierra Club calendar was two months behind. Hart lay down on the bed and closed his eyes.

Huge, irrational, fuzzy visions formed on his eyelids. He

saw Susan lying in her bed, the one set right down on the floor, someone calling to her from the next room. No. Hart tried to listen instead of think.

Someone opened the door of the bathroom, walked down the hall whistling. Hart heard someone dialing the hall phone: low, murmuring voices. And then typing, muffled, like drips of water.

After a while, the typing put him to sleep. He hadn't wanted to sleep because he thought he would dream about Susan. Instead, he had a wild dream about Ford killing him. Blowing a huge hole in his stomach with a shotgun. A hole so big Hart could put his hand through it. He didn't know how long he'd slept before Ford woke him up.

24

KEVIN WAS ON THE SIDEWALK, the snow falling on top of him, filling up his shirt collar and turning soggy when it made contact with his skin. He walked up the porch steps, shook himself off and pressed the bell with Hammer, Moss, and Foswhisher written above it. Nothing happened. Above him, he could hear laughing and a record player. He checked the name Mr. Shaw had written down and rang again. Like a dog peering around a corner, a crewcut head stuck out the door.

"Yeah," the head said.

"I'm looking for James Moss," Kevin said, not wanting to elaborate, to say that Mr. Shaw had sent him there for special help.

"O.K." The door opened full. The head was stuck on a big body, about six feet, dressed in jeans, with no shoes, the shirt open down to a dirty belly button, stuck down like an island in the white swaying fat. The beer belly yelled, "Moss — get your ass out here — some mother to see you."

Down the hall to the right, Kevin could see the living room. There were two other boys there, one on the floor fiddling with the record player and the other on a mangy mattress. The beer cans spread all around hadn't been lying on the floor long; some were still leaking their last few drops into the rug.

The record player hesitated and the guy on the mattress coaxed it, talking the record down the spindle. The needle lifted and the record hole seemed to open up. The set vibrated, the record dropped and the spindle poked straight up through the black plastic.

The girls laughed. Three girls with their shoes off. One was strutting around the room, her breasts poking out of the top of her blouse. She walked by the guy fiddling with the record player and he pulled on her arm. She collapsed on him, laughing and kicking. Kevin felt like he had when he was little and used to sneak out his father's magazines, searching through the fishing and hunting stories until he found the ones about girls hitchhiking.

The beer belly walked down the hall and stood just behind the brown-haired girl, who was leaning forward trying to pull down her short skirt. As she bent forward, the beer belly reached down under her skirt, grabbed both sides of her rear and pulled up. She howled and fell forward into the arms of the guy on the mattress.

"Don't mind them — I'm their manager."

The guy holding Kevin's arm was wiry, thin and quick, wearing slippers and real slacks, with his shirt untucked but buttoned all the way to the top.

"I'm so used to them, I don't really see them. I'm Jim

Moss." He talked fast, faster than anything Kevin had ever heard. But his words were sure, each one cut off from the rest, as if he'd prepared all his sentences in advance.

They walked down to a messy room, with bookcases on every wall, books sprawled on the floor, bed and chairs.

"It's all right for them. They have me to pull them through." Moss threw a book off the desk chair. "I wouldn't recommend it for you though."

Kevin sat on the bed on top of *Black's Law Dictionary*. He unwound his fingers from his briefcase handle and unbuttoned his coat. An electric heater whirred behind the desk.

"What do you mean, they have me to get them through?" Kevin said.

"They pay the bills and I do the studying." Moss searched around in the papers on the desk. "It's as simple as that. They almost flunked out their first year — I don't think it's too hard to see why — and I moved in. They've done all right ever since. Nothing spectacular, put passable. Anyway, they certainly will graduate." Kevin poked his tongue around the inside of his mouth.

"No cheating of course," Moss added. "I give them a lecture before each exam, and they go and take it on their own. They remember most things for a day or two. They're not stupid."

On the wall a picture of round faces, smiling in contentment, hung over golden letters that said, HARVARD LAW REVIEW. Kevin couldn't keep his eyes off the letters.

He'd seen them coming out of their white frame house, joking and talking with each other. He'd seen the way ordinary law students walked around the house looking in, wondering, wishing they had the courage to go right up to the window. The way ordinary law students tried to look like they weren't looking at all, and how that made them seem all the more intent.

"Are you really on the Law Review?" It spurted out of Kevin.

Moss's pencil hung between his thin fingers. "Not really, anymore. I don't actively participate. A pompous organization. You might say, I never really *belonged*. But don't study because of the Law Review. It'll make you too tense."

He held up a paper, tapped it lightly with the pencil.

"It says here you flunked every one of your practice exams." Kevin winced. "Defeating at first glance. I suppose that's what most people would say. But to the more trained eye, there's a certain ray of hope in it. You see, Kevin, it's against all the odds to flunk every practice exam. Even if you had done no work, at least you would have gotten a D minus from Horne. He never gives an F. Very rare. Sheer stupidity generates sympathy and is usually good for a D. No, on the whole, I'd think you made one error, the same error, on each exam."

Kevin stared at the floor, twitching.

"My God, man," Moss said, "don't look that way. You're going to be saved. I'm your ace in the hole. I can't make a Learned Hand out of you, but I can make you pass. Do you have samples of your work?"

"I've got my notes," Kevin said slowly.

"No, no, no," Moss said. "I meant an exam. But it doesn't matter." He rolled back, looking at the ceiling. "Ready?" Kevin nodded. He had his notebook open on his lap.

"Imagine an old woman comes to dinner with you," Moss said. "While you're mixing her drink, she slips on an ice cube, skates across the room, smashing your new breakfast table, demolishing it and killing herself. Got that? After you've cleaned her off the floor, you discover a statute saying homeowners must keep their land free of dangerous ice, especially, but not exclusively, ice on their sidewalks. You also find out the old woman suffered from dropsy, a falling sickness." Moss paused; he'd chewed through his pencil.

"I suppose that's enough. You're sued on two theories, one relying on the statute and the other ordinary negligence. Can they recover from you for causing the old lady's death? Can you recover the price of the breakfast table from the old bag's estate?"

Moss started to rise. "Write out an answer to that," he added. "Take about half an hour on it. Any sample will do. Bring it back a month or so before exams and we'll go over it together. Don't bother to call; just drop over."

Moss backed Kevin to the door and extended a hand. "Don't worry, there's no possibility of error in my analysis," he said as he closed the door.

Kevin walked out in the hall. The party was still going strong in the living room. When he got to the door, he saw it was two against one. One of the guys held a girl's arms and another poured beer into her mouth. It slopped down her cheeks, down her neck and into her cleavage, catching in her bra and oozing out in a dark circle over her breasts. Her skirt had ridden up over her undies as she squirmed and thrashed. Her thighs squeaked as they rubbed together. It was a clean sound like hair that's just been washed. The sweat made her bare legs shine. One of the guys reached his hand down on her stomach, right down on the panties above the crotch. She stopped laughing. Her thrashing began to have a purpose.

The beer belly knelt down beside her, grabbed her panties and started to pull them off, taking a long time, not because it was difficult, but to taunt her. The other girls were standing over him pushing on his back, telling him to go ahead.

The beer belly laughed, threw his head back and saw Kevin.

"Hey, you motherfucker," he said, "get the hell out of here."

25

AT ELEVEN O'CLOCK, Mrs. Weasal, the guardian of the Treasure Room, went to the bathroom as she'd done every night for twenty years. No one ever used the Treasure Room and there weren't any guests or tours late at night so she was able to hold to her routine steadily, through all seasons.

She looked around the room once before she pushed through the doors, then pulled her tweed suit straight because it always made her nervous to walk past the students. She noticed that the boy who'd asked her about Kingsfield's notes was sitting at the first table, but she didn't give it much thought. Anyway, he was gone when she came back.

At quarter to twelve, she put her things in her pocketbook, took one last look in the mirror and then made a thorough inspection of the room. One of the name tags on the major display case had fallen down. She picked her keys off her desk, opened the case and adjusted the card.

By the time she'd finished, it was twelve and she packed up and left, being sure to lock the door.

At one o'clock a flashlight beam ran out from under the major display case. It fluttered like a butterfly across the room and then started to run over the walls, searching among the books on the left side of the room.

"None of those books are red," Ford said. The beam turned and started across the wall facing the glass doors, working down from the top quickly.

"And they're not red, either," Ford whispered. "Maybe it's just called the Red Set; maybe it's not red at all."

The light snapped off and the room was dark again.

"Let me think," Hart said. "Let me think."

In his mind, he tried to reconstruct the entire room; he couldn't remember any set of red books. But it wouldn't be called the Red Set unless it was red. Maybe they're being bound, he thought, and cursed.

Then he remembered the door on the far side of the room. A door that grew out of the oak paneling. It wasn't a secret door; you could see the outlines.

"Wait for me," Hart said. "If I find them, I'll whistle. All right?"

"Oh sure," Ford said, "I'm just going to sit here, under the first edition of The Common Law and wait for you to whistle? Great."

Hart had already slid off into the dark, crawling across the floor in case there were guards patrolling the library reading room.

When he reached the far wall, he felt along it and found the door crack. He rose to a kneeling position and pushed. The door had no lock; it swung creaking, revealing a black void beyond. Hart whistled and shone the flashlight back over the floor so that Ford could follow.

Ford ran bent over, zigzagging between the reading tables.

"Christ's sake," Hart said. "Someone might see you. Keep down."

"I zigged," Ford said, "to avoid the bullets."

"I can feel it," Hart said, "I can feel the Red Set. I know it's here, right here."

He flicked on the light.

Around him, in neat little volumes, all red leather, were

rows of books, so close he and Ford instinctively drew back, sucked in their breath and held it.

Hart closed the door behind them and searched until he found the Kingsfield volumes. He took the first and opened to the title page: "Notes on Contracts, 1928, in a course of contracts given by Professor Williston."

"Jesus," Ford said. "The unbroken chain, the ageless passing on of wisdom, ashes to ashes, but knowledge goes on. Let's split. Now you've seen it."

Hart sat on the floor crosslegged, held the book in his lap and started turning the pages. There were dates, just like the dates in his notes and there were headings, just like his. He didn't read the words; he watched the flow of the pen over the pages. They fell on each other softly, each page knowing the idiosyncrasies of the other.

"Well," Ford said. "All right, how is it? What does it do to you?"

Hart looked up from the book, closed it and handed it up to Ford, who put it on the shelf.

"They're just notes," Hart said. "They even look like ours. I guess it was a waste of time. I don't know, I expected something more."

"Does that bother you? I mean, what did you expect?" Ford said.

"I guess nothing," Hart said. "I just thought it would be different, but I didn't know what. I wondered if he was like us."

They turned off the light and crossed the Treasure Room, figuring any watchman would be asleep by two. The doors were locked but they could open them from the inside.

"We can't leave them open," Ford said. "They'll know someone was here."

But they did leave them open because they couldn't figure out any way to close them.

"Good night, Oliver Wendell Holmes," Ford said back into the Treasure Room as they left. "Sleep well."

26

"I'D LIKE TO SEND some flowers," Hart told the man. "How do I do it?"

It was easier than he thought. He picked roses because he couldn't remember the name of any other flowers. The only difficult part was the card. He thought about it for a long time, until the shopkeeper began to look him over suspiciously. Finally, he just wrote, "Why?"

During my sophomore year in college, I wore a lumberman's shirt like Pete Seeger's and listened to Joan Baez records. When the school year ended, I went South and worked for SNCC. No one tried to kill me; no one even spit on me. I was in Mississippi. I tried to learn how to play the banjo.

I lost thirty pounds in Mississippi; I was scared all the time. I was so scared I couldn't walk the right way. Mississippi made me walk with a funny little jerk and now, five years later, I'm just beginning to walk right.

During my second year at law school we had the Harvard strike. A lot of law students came up to me during the strike and asked where the college was. I told them but I don't know if they went over.

We had some meetings at the law school during the strike. All the law professors came and talked. They talked and talked. They'd sit right down in the middle of the meetings and then raise their hands and talk. They talked for hours.

After the professors had finished talking, no one would have anything else to say and the meeting would end. We applauded the law professors after they finished talking.

Yesterday I was walking along the third floor of the new faculty office building. I was minding my own business. The Vice Dean was going back to his office. "Who are you looking for?" he yelled. I mean he yelled. I probably jumped three feet. I said I was looking for a certain professor. "He's on the fourth floor," the Vice Dean screamed. Then he shook his head and slammed the door to his office.

I thought of all the neat things I could have said: "Get fucked," or, "It's none of your business," or, "Why are you screaming at me?"

You've got to think fast to say things like that, to think of them at the time. I guess the only way to do it is to make a conscious choice and just say "Get fucked" every time the Vice Dean talks to you.

27

"I DIDN'T WANT to knock," the boy said, standing in the door of Hart's room and looking at Hart and Ford sprawled out, drunk. "I thought you might be asleep."

"What time is it?" Ford mumbled.

"Two." The boy paused, waiting for their attention. "You're both on my list. Two things. First, would you help with the mixer? Second, would you contribute to Vorgan Temby's birthday party?"

Hart decided he hated the boy. The guy was being superior because he and Ford weren't studying.

"Well, I think I can give you a definite no to the first question," Ford said. "You see, this guy and I are both queer."

"Come on," the boy said, "that's the excuse everyone in the dorms gives; we've got to get together."

"And about the birthday party," Ford went on, "I don't even know who Vorgan Temby is."

"Professor Temby." The boy glanced at Hart for support. "You know, he teaches torts. He teaches you. Look, you don't have to give, unless you want your name on the card."

"Oh," Ford said, "so that's the way it is. What do you think?"

"I think I want to think about it," Hart said. "I hate Professor Temby."

"I hate him too," the boy said. "You should make peace with people you hate."

"Not by giving them presents," Ford said. "We'll think about it."

A round face pushed through the open door.

"I'm not intruding on anything am I?" Toombs said.

"Come on in," Hart said, and the boy backed out, giving Toombs room.

"It's nothing," Toombs said. "There's just a telephone call for Hart. I thought he might want to take it."

"Why not?" she said.

Suddenly Hart was cool, the man for the situation.

"Oh, hello Susan," he said.

"I like them," she said. "It's not very original, but at least they weren't wilted. Would you like to play?"

"I'd like to talk," he said.

"We've already talked. I thought we might actually do something. You know, I don't want to sit around the apartment looking intense."

"I'd still like to talk."

"All right, forget it. Maybe we'll bump into each other in the Square."

The phone was silent, but she hadn't hung up. His strength faded.

"All right, I'd love to play," he said.

"Good." He could almost see her smiling. "Meet me at the bridge. We can walk on the other side of the river. It's quiet."

He hung up and went to his room to get his coat.

"We'll never get in," he said. The fence was fifteen feet high. Beyond it he could see the football practice fields.

"When I was in sixth grade, we had this club. We snuck into football games. Did you do things like that?"

"We rang doorbells and ran," Hart said.

After two hundred yards, the fence turned right and a row of trees pressed them against it. When they'd gone twenty yards past the bend, she turned and started through the trees.

"This is how we got in, but you've got to promise not to tell. All right?" He followed her away from the fence. They broke through the trees. An access road, plowed, shone in the moonlight. She slid down into a drainage ditch next to it.

The pipe in the ditch was about four feet high. She crouched down on the level ice floor and waddled in like a duck.

"Look," he called after her, "I'm not going into this goddamned thing." His words echoed back to him from the dark.

"I don't care what you did in first grade." He couldn't hear any answer and he stuck his head into the pipe.

"Can you hear me?" he called. "Susan!" Again, he heard his echo. He slid in like a Russian dancer, his arms wrapped around his knees.

After about thirty yards, the pipe ended in a concrete box. He felt for the top.

"You can stand up," she said from above. "Half of you is already out of the drain." He put his hands down and lifted himself onto the freezing stone floor.

"All right," he said, coughing out the grit he had filtered through his mouth. "Where is this?"

"Can you wait thirty seconds?" she said. "And don't tell me when you guess."

Moonlight came down on them from holes high above and illuminated stone pillars that stretched up where he couldn't see. They were climbing and the wind was blowing around them. A freezing wind that carried fine particles of ice. He drew the string on his parka, pulling it tight around his waist.

She stopped in an archway ahead of him. Beyond her he saw the shoulders of the football stadium, curling around on either side and then stretching out in a straight line toward the Charles River.

They were in the center of the half-circle, halfway up in the stone stands. Out the end, at the gate of the horseshoe, he could see the red chimneys of the Harvard houses. The wind swept in from the right side, coming down the stands, reversing and passing out over the football field, picking up the snow and tossing it on the seats. The moonlight made the ice pellets shine like glass beads as the wind dropped them down.

"Do you hear that?" Hart said. The wind whistled like a child blowing over a bottle. "It sounds like there are people here."

"I'm sure dopers use this place. And cats. I think someone is watching us now, plotting," she said.

A beer can bounced along the left side of the field and, carried by the wind, flew up over the retaining wall, landing in the lower stands.

"I'm freezing," he said, sitting down on the nearest seats, inviting her to wrap up in his coat.

"Don't you want to explore? We could climb to the top. You can see everything from up there." She was still standing in the archway.

"I want to talk," he said. "Besides, you must have explored this place, with other boys, since the first grade."

She sat down beside him in the stand.

"It was the sixth grade. Sixth grade. Why the hell can't you just *do things?*"

"I am trying to do something," he said into the wind.

"I'm trying to make sense. For Christ's sake, what's wrong with that? I just want us to get together."

She stood up, her hands in her pockets, and swung around so that she was looking down at him.

"One time, when Father was out of town and I was living in the house alone, I called up my aunt and asked her over for dinner. I told her it was probably the only time I'd ever be able to entertain her in style. She said, 'How sad, I always dine in style.' I didn't come here because you sent me flowers. I can always buy flowers. Hart, I could buy you. Maybe I already have."

"Eat shit," he said.

She laughed.

"At least that's more likable than trying to kill us out on the ice."

He'd lose her either way. If he did nothing, the summer would finish them.

"Hart," she said, "I like you. I really do."

"Then why the hell can't we love each other?" he shot back. "I can't live this way. I need to be organized. I need a way of living I can rationalize. This way, I spend half my time worrying. I can't work. I can't sleep. I'm going to flunk all my courses. I won't pass."

"Christ," she said, "you're the kind of person who can't help but pass. You're the kind the law school wants. Do you think anyone cares about the robots? The law school hates the guys who regulate their studying habits. The law school got them without trying. The law school wants you: the earnest ones. You've got class. The law school wants to suck out your Midwestern class. You can't flunk. That's why I'm worried about you."

"We could do things together," he moaned, "help each other, make plans, live in a sane way."

"Hell, show me something I can't buy in Langdell," she snapped. "Show me someone who doesn't kiss my father's ass. You're like a dog: you grovel or attack on command."

She backed away, toward the end of the row of seats. The darkness began to swallow her, blend her into the black stone of the stadium.

"What do you know about law school?" he called after her. "You've never been there. You couldn't get through a year at Radcliffe."

"You were born for the married students' dorm," she said from the dark. "You were born for a dating bar."

And then she was gone. He felt her go. He became part of the concrete: a leftover from the last football game. The solitary fan, waiting for spring. He'd sit all night. They'd find him in the morning, frozen.

"SUSAN."

He stood up and screamed. Looking out, he saw nothing but the empty stands and the snow. She would be through the pipe, walking home.

"Susan," he said, just loud enough to lift the word around him into the wind. He wondered what it was going to be like to cry.

"Did you think I was going out through the tunnel alone?" she said from the darkness behind him. Her hand brushed his shoulder.

28

DOWN IN FRONT, the students who raised their hands battled out a question of law for Kingsfield. It was as though they were one person, their minds one mind. Hart made a point, and then sat back, watching the others move around his assertion, cutting off the loose edges. He was locked into the graceful movement of the argument.

Above them, Kingsfield regulated, nodding approval, and every now and then, when enthusiasm overcame logic, taking possession of an irregular thought and squashing it.

The discussion was close to resolution. Its lines were about to converge when Kingsfield stopped them. "All right," he said, "that's enough." He looked down, unbuttoned his coat, pulled out his gold watch and checked the time.

Hart looked at the others. It was as though all the people who had been talking were frozen: mouths still open, hands still raised, pens poised over notebooks. They were on the edge of bursting out, continuing the argument in spite of Kingsfield.

"We always seem to hear from the same people," Kingsfield said. "Would someone who has not contributed care to speak? Someone who usually does not raise his hand?"

Hart sighed. No one would raise his hand. A hand up would be an admission that normally the hand was not raised. An admission that one was a coward. This was taking up time. They might not finish the discussion.

"I suppose I'll have to ferret you out then," Kingsfield said, looking irritated because, as always, there were no new volunteers. "Mr. Brooks, will you give the facts of *Tinn* versus *Hoffmann?*"

Kevin looked surprised and scared. Like most of the class, he'd retired into his private thoughts while the regulars floated in the higher reaches of the law.

"Right," Kevin said, turning the pages of his book, trying to find *Tinn* v. *Hoffmann.*

The case was complicated: some thirteen letters and telegrams between a company wanting to sell pig iron and a company wanting to buy it. Every time it looked like they'd finally made a deal, the buyer backed down, hedged. Finally, the frustrated seller gave up and sold the pig iron elsewhere. Now the buyer was suing, saying that the seller had promised to give him the iron.

"Mr. Brooks," Kingsfield asked, "how was the case decided, and how does the decision relate to what we've been discussing?"

"Right," Kevin said again, and paused.

Hart put his hand up, swung it like an ax reaching the apogee of its arch. His eyes pleaded with Kingsfield. It wasn't fair to stop them so close to wrapping it all up.

Hart was ignored. His stomach muscles tightened. He saw the wall clock moving toward ten. *Tinn* v. *Hoffmann* was the crux of the whole thing.

"In the first letter of November twenty-eight," Kevin said, "we find this phrase, 'make you an offer.' The court seemed to stress this phrase. No, I guess that's not the crucial passage." Kevin wavered.

The correct answer tried to push open Hart's mouth. Kingsfield seemed to sense it and, as though he'd known all along, he called on Hart.

"Really!" Hart exploded, drowning out Kevin's lingering voice. "The correct rule, and the one along which this case was decided, is: In an ambiguous set of facts, the party who creates the ambiguity and tries to use it to his own advantage shall have the ambiguity resolved against him."

The rest of the regulars stuck their hands up. They started to elaborate on Hart's point. Kingsfield glanced quickly at Hart. There was no smile, but the look was enough. It was a recognition of Hart's seat, a token for a job well done.

Hart looked toward the window and saw Kevin, slouched

down behind his book. What the hell was wrong with Kevin? He'd given Kevin the answer, but Kevin wasn't taking advantage of it.

As Hart watched, Kevin's hands began to shake. Kevin put down the book and gripped the desk, holding onto the curving bench top like a sailor clinging to a spar. "Fuck," Hart said under his breath, "fuck."

After class, Hart walked out on the stone steps of Langdell. He could see the entire yard. Law students were rushing between classes. All of them using the same jerking motion that stressed they were going somewhere important. It was the same pace they used in the Square. Only there, for some reason, it looked silly. Hart would see them toting their casebooks as if they were going to a board meeting. And then he'd see them again, twenty minutes later, still circling the Square, looking for girls or spying on the college. The first time you saw a law student in the Square, he might wave. The second time, he'd plunge into the crowd, hiding.

The yard had gotten a clean coat of snow last night. Most people stuck to the path and, except for the occasional trail of a dog, the snow was unbroken, a solid reflecting mirror that threw the light up onto Langdell. The light seemed to stick there, held by tiny pieces of quartz in the granite. It was one of the few times the immensity of the building made sense. It rose from the white blanket like a sparkling ice wall.

There were girls on the paths. Radcliffe girls heading back to the dorms, and only crossing through the law school because it was the most direct route. Radcliffe girls forced there because it was winter and cold. They kept away from the law students.

A group of professors came up the stairs, heading for their

classes. Hart drew to the side of the steps, away from the huge door. The professors hung together as they climbed, marching in formation, and the students shrank away, letting them pass. A boy at the top of the steps opened the door for them. They seemed to expect that and did not break step.

Far off to the right a law student got out of a V.W. station wagon. His wife slid into the driver's seat and handed him his briefcase. They didn't kiss before she drove away.

Even with the sun, Hart began to get cold. There were more students on the steps now and he began to feel pulled by them. He took a last look over the yard, at the final stragglers moving toward Langdell, and retreated into the building.

29

"Where's O'Connor?" Bell said, looking around the table. It was at least thirty minutes after the time they were supposed to start.

"I'm afraid that O'Connor's decided to cut back and cut out the study group," Anderson said. "Needless to say, his loss is our gain."

Kevin looked agitated. His face started to shake.

"What'll we do about his outline? People shouldn't quit the group. Jesus, what the hell will we do at the end of the year. We're supposed to help each other."

"Shut up, will you Kevin," Bell said. "I never liked O'Connor. I don't give a shit about his outline. He's a little pimp. I wasn't going to share my outline with him anyway."

"You what!" Kevin said. He stood up, pushing back his chair. "We've got to stick together. That's the whole point of this group."

"The point of this group is to learn the law," Anderson said matter-of-factly. "And O'Connor never was much help. By the way, one might say the same of you."

Kevin sat down.

"There isn't anything we can do about it," Hart said, glancing at Ford. "Maybe O'Connor will come back. Who knows? It's his right to leave. Jesus, don't you think so?"

Ford nodded. He was looking down at the table.

"We can all do some of O'Connor's work," Ford said. "We'll just divide up his course. But one thing. Let's not get soft-hearted. O'Connor is out and that's it. He doesn't get our outlines at the end of the year and we don't get his."

"Listen," Hart said, "Let's not make any rules yet. Maybe O'Connor will come back tomorrow."

"Yes," Kevin said, "I'll talk to him. Someone's got to talk to him. People can't quit the group."

30

HART DRANK half a bottle of scotch with Ford and he still couldn't sleep. He got up, turned on the light and started to read again. It was slow going. Numbed by the scotch, he made fifteen pages in four hours.

When it got to be light, his vision stopped functioning. He set his alarm and pulled the sheet over him to get an hour's sleep in before contracts.

He fell asleep thinking about Susan.

Hart woke up at ten. At first, he didn't believe it. He ran out into the hall. It was silent, empty except for a janitor sweeping at the far end.

"SHIT . . . SHIT . . . SHIT."

Hart screamed and the janitor turned around, gave Hart a glance, decided Hart was crazy and went on sweeping.

Hart ran back to his room. He shook his watch. It still read ten o'clock. He slammed his palm against his head, blinked his eyes and looked out the window. The last stragglers were going into Langdell. He'd missed contracts but he could still salvage torts.

He pulled on his pants, his shirt, put on his shoes without worrying about socks, grabbed his parka, his books, and ran out the door, down the stairs, flying toward the granite monolith.

Through the small windows in the door, he could see the German professor at the lectern and a boy in a seat near where Hart should have been sitting, answering a question.

He'd have to walk down through the class to get to his seat. He sucked in air; he could do it. He'd look down at the floor and concentrate on something else. The German professor might not even notice him.

His casebook was in his right hand and he shifted it to the left. It was red. It should have been blue. Blue was torts. Red was contracts. He'd grabbed the wrong book. He backed away from the door, cursing.

Susan opened the door, dressed in jeans. She smiled when she saw him.

"Why, Mr. Hart," she said. "Are you on vacation from the law school? I should think you have classes."

"I canceled class," he yelled. His hair, unbrushed, stuck up in the air. He hadn't buckled his belt and it had worked loose, hanging down.

"Why, Mr. Hart," she said, "you have a tail!" She bent down, picked up the trailing end of the belt and handed it to him. "There," she said, "now you're back in one piece."

"I missed class," he screamed. "I missed class because I can't get my goddamned mind together with you giving me so much bullshit. I missed it because you won't let us lead any kind of organized life."

"Us?" she said. "Mr. Hart, I agree you need organization." She looked him up and down. "But, US?"

"I missed contracts, Susan."

"Screw contracts," she said, turning away. He kept standing there, holding his belt. Then he heard her banging around in the kitchen.

He followed the sound.

"What are you doing?" He tried so hard to control the sound of his voice that his words were only a forced whisper. He sat down at the kitchen table. One of the legs didn't reach the floor and it tilted when he put his arms down.

"Breakfast," she said.

"Well, give me some," he snapped, hanging his head down over the table. "Or is that too organized?"

She picked a bowl from the sink, blew in it to make it dry and dropped it on the table. It banged around in a circle before settling in front of him. Then she flipped a piece of shredded wheat from the waist. It flew toward him like a Frisbee, and he pulled away. The bowl caught it. He looked down, crumpled it with his fingers. It came apart at the first touch and he saw dust rising out of the bowl.

"Do you have any milk?" he demanded.

"Oh," she said, her eyes getting big and her mouth rounding out, "you want the deluxe breakfast. Well, I'm so glad you said so."

She opened the icebox; it tilted forward but held. Leaving a full carton on the shelf, she picked out a glass of milk, crusted with old cream, lifted the glass to her shoulder and sighted down, letting the milk slop from three feet.

"One deluxe breakfast for the hungry man," she called toward the far wall, as if there were another room back there. "One, hot tot, deluxe, superior, top-drawer breakfast . . . oh go fuck yourself."

The milk slid over the rim of the bowl, spattered onto the table, leaked through Hart's shirt, and spread itself around his elbows.

He jumped up, shook the milk off his arms.

"Now get this," she said. "I want you out of here. And I don't want you to ever come in here and scream at me again. But I'll just settle for having you out."

He backed into the living room, watched her through the door sponging up the milk. She didn't look in his direction again and he left.

His belt fell off on the landing. But he didn't notice.

31

BELL HAD OBVIOUSLY lost touch with his surroundings. He wasn't in contracts class, but in a courtroom leading the defense. It was as though he'd been galvanized by the portraits of old judges hung around the room and was arguing his case to them.

"These deadman statutes are unfair," Bell said, speaking slowly and ponderously. "For the life of me, I can't understand why the judge felt he had to follow them. They don't give a plaintiff the chance to testify."

Thirty seats to Bell's left, Hart was rubbing the little metal tag stuck to his particular section of the curving desk top. The tag read 259. Not a bad number, Hart thought, but not a great one either. A pretty average seat, not too far back, nor too far forward.

Hart was bored. Bell was on the right track but he didn't say it right. He was too pompous. The deadman statutes — which forbid a plaintiff suing an estate from testifying in certain situations — were unjust. But Bell should get on to the ways of bypassing the statutes.

"It's not justice," Bell said ominously. "Why, take *Proctor* versus *Proctor*. The girl had worked for her aunt for ten years because the aunt had promised to leave her the house. I say the girl should get the house since she worked for it. It's a crummy technicality that says she can't testify. It isn't fair."

Kingsfield glanced absent-mindedly down at the seating chart. The seating chart would list 259, and under it, Hart's name. The number given Hart in a small brown unmarked paper packet at the beginning of the year. He wondered who assigned him the number. There must be some little man, locked away in the guts of Langdell. But why did he give him 259?

"Let's see," Kingsfield said. "Your name was Bell?"

"That's right," Bell said. "Bell, as in Liberty Bell."

"Did it ever occur to you, Liberty Bell was it? Did it ever occur to you that the courts didn't write the deadman statutes? That the legislature did? That the court is bound to follow the legislature?"

There goes the bait, Hart thought. Now Bell should say yes, the court should follow the legislature, but there are ways of getting around the deadman statutes, ways which do not warp the statute itself. In fact, there are seventeen ways.

Hart swung his hand up. If Bell wouldn't answer, he would. He'd had enough of Bell anyway. Bell was sounding like God. The students around Hart noticed the hand but looked down toward the podium in silence, ignoring him.

Jesus, Hart thought, don't they want a better answer? Don't they want to know? And then he realized that they didn't want a better answer, and he lowered his hand slowly to his desk.

Kingsfield sensed the silence the class expected him to fill. In an almost resigned voice, he said, "I think, Mr. Bell, I shall avoid the privilege of ringing you further."

The class broke loose, roared, rocked back in their seats convulsed, ignoring the fact that the joke was stale and trite. Bell looked confused. He hadn't gotten the point that one should laugh with people, at oneself, and then people will cease to laugh at you.

The laughter of the class merged with the sound of the students in the back getting out of their seats. The hour had ended. Hart raced to the front of the classroom.

"Bell was right about the deadman statutes," he called up to Kingsfield in a worried voice. "There are at least seventeen ways to get around the deadman statutes. You wrote an article showing that."

Kingsfield peered down from behind the lectern, looking at Hart like a jeweler examining a watch through his eyepiece.

"If I wrote an article stating there were seventeen ways to get around deadman statutes, then I don't need to be told Mr. Bell was correct," Kingsfield said. "Is there anything else?"

Kingsfield picked up his books and put them under his arm. He put a hand on the lectern and half turned toward the door. Hart was still standing silently below him.

"What is your name?" Kingsfield said absent-mindedly.

What was his name? Jesus, was it a trick? A way of putting him down?

"Mr. Hart," Hart said.

"Well, Mr. Hart, I can understand your wanting to ride to the rescue of the unfortunate Mr. Bell," Kingsfield said, smiling slightly. "But it is a little late now, isn't it? After all, you had your chance in class. No one stops you from expressing yourself."

Hart turned away. He took a step toward the aisle leading back to his seat.

"Wait a minute," Kingsfield said. "I've got a proposition for you."

Hart stopped. He looked up at the lectern with a confused stare.

"I need a student to research a subject for me. I usually choose second and third year students but you seem to know your stuff. Interested?"

Hart froze while the enormity of what the professor had said sank in.

"It's just background work. You merely research a topic for me and then summarize your findings in a paper. It gives you a chance to do some written work and, of course, aids me. Well?"

"Sure," Hart said, gradually melting into an embarrassed euphoria.

"Come by my office this afternoon. My secretary will give you a data sheet listing the subject. Don't make the paper too long. Perhaps ten pages. I'll expect it in about a week."

With that Kingsfield jumped through his little door and was gone.

32

HART DECIDED from the beginning it would be an exceptional paper. He resolved to follow every reference which the major cases made to the minor cases. He resolved to read every Law Review article on the subject, comb every statute.

He began with a tremendous burst of energy. It seemed that nothing could tire him as he madly filled up three-by-five index cards with the facts of the cases. At the end of three days, he had over four hundred of these cards, all sitting neatly in a special metal file box.

Then he started to write. It did not go well. He decided that the problem lay in not having sufficiently dominated his sources and he went back to the library for more research. At the end of five days he had to buy another file box.

The night before he was to hand the paper in, he cursed himself for thinking he could have done so much. He wished he'd started small and worked like a jeweler. He saw that his mistake lay at the very beginning when he'd tried to do more than he could to please Kingsfield. He stayed up all night, trying to organize his eight hundred cards into a logical sequence and, by five, as the first light was coming to the law school yard, he knew that he would not finish.

He cursed himself again, looked at his casebooks, at the masses of assigned classroom work he had not done, and wished he'd never taken the project.

Perhaps he should go and tell Kingsfield. He went to the window, looked at Langdell and gave up that thought. He'd take an extra week. Of course Kingsfield would be mad because the paper was late. But he wouldn't tell him about it. He'd wait until the end of the second week, until Kingsfield was sure the paper would never be finished and then surprise the professor, present him with a supreme piece that would delight him and justify the tardiness.

Hart got happy again, thinking about his solution to his troubles. When the library door opened, he raced in, filled with new energy. To make up for the week's delay, he upped his standards. That called for more research. He bought another file box. But he wouldn't be caught short. Not again. He worked in two shifts, staying in the library during the day, and then, at night, typing in his room.

He typed until he had to uncurl his fingers in the morning to hold his pencil in the library. The typed sheets grew, rattling themselves off the machine at the rate of six an hour. At the end of three days, he had piled up more than two hundred pages which sat on his desk, mocking him, because they had no logical order.

It got hard to stay awake. He bought NoDoz and it made his hands shake. He had to print his notes to make them legible. His production began to fall behind. He bought instant coffee and made it from the hot water tap in the bathroom. His face got a warm patina of caked sweat and ink. Finally, five days into the second week, he had a vision that he would fail.

His arms broke out in sweat and he tried to redouble his efforts, forcing the tiredness out of him. He locked himself in his room, alone with the typewriter. He sat and typed. Gradually, his mind blurred over. He concentrated on his first pages, hoping that if he got that right, everything else would follow. Finally, losing his objectivity in the confines of the tiny cell, and knowing it, he concentrated on his first sentence, trying to make at least one permanent block from which he could build the rest.

On the last night of the second week he knew he could not hand it in. The paper was unorganized, hopelessly long, badly typed. He sat for a long time, too nervous to sleep and too tired to work. Finally, he figured that if the paper was already a week late, another week would make no difference. He slept fitfully for two hours and then rose to begin again.

This time it was different. He knew that to justify this

111

extra week, the paper would have to be even better. And he knew, though he did not admit it, that no paper could be that good. He grew more tired, until at the end of two weeks and five days, nothing seemed to matter anymore.

He had reached a sort of watershed in his existence, a balancing point in his mind where the unquestioned assumptions he'd started with withered to nothing. The thought of actually telling Kingsfield that he had not done, and could not do, the paper had been a thought so terrible he had not admitted its possibility. Now, one more visit to the library, typing one more word, was worse. He had not slept for four days.

On his way to Kingsfield's office, he wondered if he had really known long before, perhaps a week ago, that it would end this way. He wondered if he had secretly kept going in order to reach this state of tiredness so that he would be able to face Kingsfield.

Kingsfield's outer office was deserted. The room trembled slightly as though the walls were waiting for the imminent arrival of a great many people. Hart walked to the electric typewriter sitting on a metal desk that guarded the oak door to the inner office. The typewriter was warm and resting his hand on it, he knew that the trembling was merely the machine, left running. He flicked a button and the room was silent.

"May I help you?" a girl at the door asked. He pulled his hand off the typewriter. As she walked across the room the string of pearls dangling over her baby blue sweater lapped on the books piled in her arms. She snuggled in behind the desk, swiveling back and forth, moving her hips into the desk crevice. Then she looked up at Hart and jumped.

Instead of shrinking under the stare, he welcomed it. She

was looking at the stained white shirt he had not taken off for a week, the inky hands and the disheveled hair. Hart rolled back on his heels, glad that the effort he had put out was apparent. At least Kingsfield would know he'd tried.

"May I help you?" she said again.

"I have to see Professor Kingsfield," Hart said, half closing his eyes. "It will only take a minute."

She used the phone, talking so low he could not hear, and then told him to go in. Hart walked to the great oak door, put his hand on the bronze knob and took a deep breath. For a second, he thought about leaving, going back and trying again. Then he opened the door.

His feet were covered by a thick green carpet, stretching out before him, rolling down like a field between the dark bookcases, down to a huge plate glass window taking up the entire rear of the room. At a large glossy desk in front of the window sat Kingsfield.

"Come in," Kingsfield snapped, pointing toward a leather armchair in front of the desk. Hart walked to the chair and sat. His fingerprints sweated into the chair's leather arms. He folded his hands in his lap. Kingsfield continued shuffling through the papers on his desk top for perhaps two minutes.

Finally, the professor's thick white eyebrows came to the top of his glasses frames. "What do you want?" he said.

"I couldn't do the paper," Hart said. He hesitated, on the verge of pouring it all out. Kingsfield rocked back in his chair. Suddenly the balance tipped the other way. In a burst of moral responsibility — a feeling that he owed more than he could repay, that Kingsfield had trusted him and he'd destroyed that trust — Hart decided that he would finish the paper.

"I need more time," Hart said quickly, forgetting the

library and how much he hated his typewriter. "Just a couple of days. Really. I can get it done soon. Maybe in two days. Maybe tomorrow."

Kingsfield looked out the window.

"I've done all the basic work," Hart added. "All I need is some time to put it together. I even have a draft." As he said it, his stomach turned over. He was lying, calling it a draft, but he couldn't stop himself.

"I don't think that will be necessary," Kingsfield said. "I appreciate your telling me the paper is not done."

Hart sank back into his chair. Kingsfield was letting him off. Jesus. It was something else to add to the moral scale. Now he had to finish.

"I can do it," Hart said.

"It isn't necessary," Kingsfield said.

"It won't be hard," Hart said.

"When your paper was three days late, I had someone else do it," Kingsfield snapped. "It was only a background piece. Data for my own work. As you see, your contribution isn't necessary."

The professor looked off again, back toward the window.

"One more thing," he said, not turning. "You ought to get some sleep."

Hart walked out. He did not say anything to the secretary.

33

KEVIN TRUDGED toward the law school. Once or twice he missed the path in the dark and his foot fell six inches into the soft snow. That would slow him down and he'd check his watch. His book was due back at the library before midnight.

Before he got to the yard he heard the music, loud and out of tune even for a mixer. Harkness was off the direct route to Langdell but he walked by, peeking in from the lawn at the dancers. Law students are the world's worst, he thought. Caught right in between: too old to let go and too young to foxtrot. They compromised, stood still, swinging their arms. He knew he could do better.

He pressed his face against the window. A black girl in front of the band danced in a fringed skirt. He remembered reading somewhere about burlesque girls tying tassels on their nipples. When he looked at his watch again, it was past twelve and the library had closed. He walked into Harkness.

Inside, down the stairs, a greasy dorm committee member was selling tickets, arguing with a student.

"You going in?" the greasy seller asked the student. "It'll cost you a dollar, if you have your dorm card." Kevin peeked in past them, watching the black girl.

"I've got to find my roommate," the student said to the ticket seller. "It's important."

"Let's have the band announce it," the seller said.

"Oh no," the student said, turning to go. "It's just his mother. She has cancer, you know. Nothing serious. He can call the hospital in the morning."

As the ticket seller moved off to catch the student, Kevin slipped in. He melted into the back with the boys around the dance floor. He'd just stand there and watch. There wasn't anything wrong with that. The band was building on one chord, gradually increasing the amplification. The note seemed to give the pulsing blue lights a thickness that covered Kevin, wrapping him up with the people around him.

The girls were inside: a concentric but smaller circle. Some looked like the girls Kevin had seen walking in the

Square. Little girl dresses coming down just over the crotch and tied in under their breasts. Slinky fabrics that stuck to them. Others were prehistoric and familiar, a little like Asheley. Not a trace of the braless children who bounced like balls along the sidewalks around the Square. Like polished stones on a bracelet they stood in nervous little groups, not a bead among them. A-lined skirts, matching sweaters, low-heeled shoes. And to finish it off, maybe a scarf or a gold pin.

He felt comfortable. At home the clothes might be a little more starched, a little more hick. But basically it was the same. He wondered where this group came from. Not from Radcliffe. They were a scrapbook, a page from *Mademoiselle*. He began to feel alive and walked over to get a drink, leaving his briefcase on a chair.

He hadn't danced in so goddamned long. Asheley didn't like to dance now. She thought people could tell about the baby. But out there was a herd of maybe fifty girls. All he had to do was go up to one, stick out his hand and grab. He tried to remember what he'd said, back there before Harvard Law School. "Would you like to dance?" Not very compelling. "Say, baby, let's, ah, you know, go and dance?" No. He thought about the apartment and how they'd fixed it up like her parents' house. How Asheley had made pillows for the sofa.

A girl wearing a blue skirt and matching cardigan backed toward him, making room for the dancers. Her hair had streaked blond stripes and her hands, clasped behind her back, wore a gold charm bracelet. The band was coming to its maximum loudness, finishing with the chord, letting the electric guitars make their own music so that you felt you were in a car about to crash.

She kept backing and he tried to move away. A circle of boys blocked him. Then she was there, her head only a foot away, her hands in front of him. She hit and swung around.

Her face wasn't half bad, a kind of puckered fresh face, like she'd washed it with Lavoris. She was switching from one foot to another and he read the signals as clearly as if she had actually spoken to him: Dance with me, all my girl friends are dancing, I'm not half bad, really. He went blank and couldn't move. Then he nodded toward the dance floor and took her hand.

It took a few seconds to readjust, to plant his feet, start shaking his body. A few seconds to get so that he didn't care how he looked and danced by himself away from everyone. He got it finally and it felt good. He let himself go with the lights and the music, turning his mind away from the law school.

The band stopped, about to do a new number or a continuation of the old one. Who could tell? She was facing away from him but tapping out code with her fingers: You can take me back, but I'd like to keep dancing. I'm O.K., really.

The band played slow. The boys who were afraid to dance fast started looking for girls. Kevin whisked her out, put his face down on her neck and tingled with the knowledge that he was touching her.

The strobe light flickered and he thought he saw Ford. He dodged over to where the band was, tried to keep his face out of sight. In the move, his right arm slid around her, pulling her close, touching the outside of her breast. His hand shook as she nestled in.

"I've got to get out of here," he whispered, but he didn't let go her arm and while he crept through the shadows she stayed with him.

*   *   *

117

Anderson came up behind Hart, tapped him on the back and waved good-bye. The library would close in an hour, and Anderson was getting out early.

Hart had made his mind up to begin reading again when someone coughed. The tables, big slabs stuck out from the walls like docked ships, threw the noise up forty feet to the vaulted ceiling rimmed with gold and then the sound fell back, touching every corner of the room.

Though Hart had been at the table for three hours, he'd gotten very little done. The girls' laughter as they were led from the mixer to the dorm, not the rock music, had driven Hart from his room. Hollow, forced laughter. The sentence Hart was looking at faded like all the others, lost in a museum of citation and detail.

". . . Sir, you cited *Hennig* versus *Dorstal Radiation* as 321 OS 435; isn't the correct citation 322 OS 435?"

". . . I cited what as what?"

". . . Please, sir, I want some more."

"Mr. Limbkins, I beg your pardon, sir! Oliver Twist has asked for more!"

"For *more!*"

Hart saw Kingsfield walking to the edge of the podium, his eyes fixed, glaring. Hart saw Kingsfield explode with distant and uncommon authorities. Saw himself falling into a quicksand of cases. He saw his exam, with a nice rosy F on top of it.

"Good try, Hart, you'll get the hang of it sometime."

"I'm sorry, Professor Kingsfield, I didn't know you were there."

"Good try, Hart."

"I want you, professor, I want you."

The library lights flickered, signaling it was ten minutes

118

till closing time. Ford closed his book and threw a wadded piece of paper at Hart. When Hart moved, he saw his hand had sweated through his paper, ruining a page of notes.

They walked out together and then took turns opening the tunnel doors. Passing the telephone, Hart shuddered.

"Why don't you call her?" Ford said. "What the hell. This is a lousy night for studying."

"No," Hart said, "I can't."

"For God's sake, why not? If you can't do anything else, call her and beg. I would."

"No," Hart said. "I can't. Anyway, she doesn't like begging."

"What does she like?"

"Forget it, will you. She doesn't like nuts. Anyway it's not her. I don't want to call her."

A student wearing a jacket and tie came into the hall. They heard laughter from the student's room as he staggered toward the bathroom, holding a glass. There were screams from a room further down the hall.

"Let's go," Ford said. "Let's get something to eat."

"Yeeeeeeooooooweeeeeee . . . ."

Hart screamed into the night and jumped off the dorm steps, landing face down in the snow which muffled the last part of the scream. But it was half-hearted and lying there he felt as bad as he had before he jumped.

"You're feeling good?" Ford asked, his hands stuck down in the fleece of his Antartex.

"No," Hart said from the snow bank. "It's the snow, I don't know."

He pulled himself up and brushed off his parka. He'd

gotten it at home. A big, quilted, dacron-filled jacket. Red so it could be used hunting, which Hart never did. With six pockets tucked under the seams and both buttons and a zipper. It was the nicest thing he owned.

With a hand on Ford's shoulder for balance, Hart knocked his boots against the steps. He liked the solid way they hit. The buildings should be hills and he and Ford should be going hiking.

They crossed the freshman yard onto the sidewalk of the main street and waited for a break in the traffic. The light turned red. A shiny Corvette stopped and an old Volkswagen gently skidded into the Corvette's rear end. They crossed in front of the cars. The drivers had jumped out and were screaming at each other.

"Sue the bastard!" Ford yelled when they reached the safety of the opposite sidewalk.

They stopped in front of a sandwich shop. Inside the plate glass window, Hart saw milling people. He and Ford sat at the counter, alongside an Indian couple. Not American Indians, but Indians from India. The girl wore a sari and over it a heavy woolen coat two sizes too big. The Indian got a hamburger for his girl and offered her the ketchup as if it were a present.

Then the hamburger was gone.

Hart swiveled around. On the sidewalk this guy, maybe six feet tall, held the hamburger against the window and flipped the bird. It took Hart and Ford a while to understand that he'd come in and actually stolen a hamburger. People began to turn around.

"How about that?" Ford said. "How about that?"

The Indian girl cowered behind her man, who was mumbling something that Hart thought was maybe a Hindu prayer. The prayer had no effect. The guy still stood there

— not running or even looking like he was going to run — and flipping the bird.

"I'll be damned," Ford said, and turned back to the counter. Other people were turning too, as if the event was over, and soon Hart was the only one still facing out.

"I'm going to talk to him," Hart said. "Order me a cheeseburger."

Ford grabbed at the red parka.

"No, that's not . . ."

But Hart was gone, zipping up his parka and sliding his hands down into his pockets.

"Why'd you take it?"

The guy turned when he heard Hart's voice. He was taller than Hart had thought and wearing a yellow windbreaker with some kind of insignia on it.

"Waddyamean?"

"The hamburger." Hart smiled, moving closer. "Why'd you take it?"

"Youwannit?"

The hamburger fell beneath the boy's legs. He straddled it and swung out in a huge arc. Hart couldn't get his hands out of his pockets. The fist smacked down along his forehead, his feet slid on the ice and he fell over.

"He's crazy," Ford said from nowhere, pulling Hart by his shoulder, watching the yellow windbreaker and, for some reason, the hamburger in the snow.

Inside, the Indian girl had another hamburger. People were sitting where Ford and Hart had sat.

"Let's go," Ford said. "Hell, you're blocking the sidewalk."

For a second, it looked as if they would go. Hart half turned toward Ford. But then, as Ford moved ahead, Hart seemed to detonate backward, turning in the air like a diver coming off a board. The boy swung as the red flashed toward him and his fist sank deep into the dacron, missing Hart's body.

All one hundred and fifty pounds of Hart landed like shrapnel. One arm locked around the guy's neck, one knee tucked in, slamming into the guy's chest, and the other leg, trailing, gave Hart a final kick off the ground — propelling him up as if he were climbing a wall.

The force knocked them back together. Like dancers they hit the window and were sprung back out by the recoil of the glass. Hart landed on top. His fists slammed into the windbreaker, caving it in like a dying air mattress.

"Yashee," the boy screamed — meaning you shit, but the words blending together in a cry. And then he gurgled as Hart's fist came down, mashing his tongue into his teeth. Womp: Hart's elbows like pistons landing in the fat.

The guy rose off the ground, pulling Hart with him, as if the force of Hart's blows were driving hand holes in the yellow windbreaker and the stomach it covered.

They grabbed Hart's arms and started to pull him back. "NOT HIM, NOT HIM, THE OTHER ONE, THE OTHER ONE," Ford screamed. But too late and before they let him go the guy got in one blow alongside Hart's nose and then collapsed back into the snow like an overturned garbage can.

Hart saw they had been fighting in the street. The lights of the honking cars frightened him. Ford steadied him and led him away.

"Listen, they might run over him," Hart said. "We've got to get him out of the street."

"They are," Ford said. "For Christ's sake."

And then they were away from the Square and into the quiet Cambridge streets and old houses.

"Do you want the hamburger?" Ford said. "I picked it up while you were fighting."

"No, you can have it," Hart mumbled.

"It's pretty cold," Ford said, and dropped the hamburger on a doorstep. "How do you feel?"

He felt all right. That was the surprising thing. He actually felt slightly better.

"O.K.," he said, moving closer to Ford. "I don't feel all that stupid."

"You're going to feel lousy tomorrow, you crazy ass. Your face will puff up like a balloon and your muscles will ache for a week."

"That's O.K.," Hart said.

"You know," Ford said, "I'm really glad I got to know you. I don't want you to think this is sentimental. I mean, you're crazier than hell."

Kevin sat across from her, not knowing what to say and not saying anything. He was scared and churning. They were so close in the room, almost on top of each other. Her on the chair and him on the bed. The clutter of her things — bottles of cosmetics, posters and pictures — made the room seem smaller than Hart's and Ford's rooms at the law school. Hart and Ford, he thought. He heard a girl laughing down the hall.

"I'm studying to be a teacher," she said. "You stay here for two years and then go somewhere else." He nodded.

Her legs were huge. He hadn't noticed, dancing with her. Looking down on them they seemed thin because of the angle. But with her across from him it was different, and he saw they had no taper, and that she knew it too because she tried to hide them one behind the other.

She leaned forward, trying to push the legs back. It

123

brought her close and he knew that just by sitting there, not saying anything because he was scared out of his mind, he was making her lose ground. It made him aware of everything he did.

She pulled on the blue knit sweater. It looked like she'd bought it because of an ad, not wanting to confirm what she must have known: that it was too small, made her wrists stick out long and thick. The charms tinkled. She was fighting the silence.

"What would you like to do?" she asked. "I don't have any dope." He looked toward the posters on the walls. She shuffled, rearranging herself, taking advantage of the reprieve from his eyes.

"Maybe we should go back," she said. "I mean, there really isn't much to do here. Do you want to go back?"

His eyes traveled around the walls before they came to her. She tightened as they moved, drew together, waiting for him. The knowledge that the balance was so much in his favor shook him, forced him. He had it now. He might go through the rest of his life and never have it again. The baby would finish it.

He looked to the right and she looked with him, worrying about which decoration had caught his eye. He put out his hand in the blind spot her eyes left, reached her face, curled his fingers around her neck. He didn't let her look up and stop him with an expression. He moved her head forward to his chest, reached his arms around her, pulling her off the chair and onto the bed. Kept her head tucked in, her face away from him. She came like she was almost glad. Like she'd rather hide under him than let him inspect her.

Reaching down, his mind wasn't clear and it got worse. It was only the times she moved, tried to stop him, that he remembered it wasn't Asheley.

SPRING

34

KINGSFIELD SLAMMED his hand down on the lectern and the lectern amplified the sound, holding it in its wooden heart and then booming the noise across the room as if someone had fired a shot in the mountains. Hart snapped to attention. Kingsfield had called on the student directly to Hart's right.

It was unsettling to have someone so near answering a question. It put Hart into Kingsfield's peripheral vision. Along with the other students near the boy, Hart bent down over his book and started preparing the next case.

He tried to look unconcerned yet attentive as he read. It was important to look unconcerned. Kingsfield fell on nervousness like a tick.

The professor slammed the lectern again and involuntarily Hart's head snapped back. Kingsfield had called on the student directly to Hart's left. Hart began to read in earnest. Obviously, Kingsfield was focusing on Hart's area. The facts of the next case formed in his mind. He relaxed slightly. He'd be ready if Kingsfield called on him.

Perhaps it had been a mistake to sit in his seat. In the morning before class, Hart had gone walking, splashing through puddles, exulting in the good weather. The walk had taken him to Susan's and he'd stood outside her building hoping she might come down. If he'd sat in the back, he could have thought about her.

Kingsfield slapped the lectern, canceling the lifeless answer of the student to Hart's left. All right, Hart thought, call on someone on the other side of the room. You've soaked the students here. But Kingsfield called on the student directly in front of Hart. The boy started to answer reluctantly and badly.

Hart slumped, uneasy because he'd jumped when the student had been called on. What the hell was Kingsfield doing? It was as if the professor were circling him, drawing a tight ring around his seat. Hart's body began to ache, solidify into a rigid position.

He tried to bring the facts of the next case to mind. The facts slipped away from him. Was that it? Was Kingsfield trying to scare him into forgetting the facts? And then, once he'd forgotten, nail him before the class?

No, he told himself, stop thinking crazy things. It's just luck that Kingsfield has called on the students around you. Even so, Hart glanced at the clock, wishing it would hurry to ten. Go, clock, he said, get your ass to ten.

Kingsfield's index finger chopped the air, as if he were drawing an imaginary red line down an imaginary paper. He dispatched the student in front of Hart. Hart braced. Kingsfield was looking at him. With a supreme effort, Hart was able to recall the facts of the next case. He could answer.

Kingsfield called on the student behind Hart. Like a knife thrower, Kingsfield had tagged the students around Hart but left the center inviolate.

Hart began to sweat. The cases he'd carefully prepared dissolved. Jesus, what had he done? No one called on students in a circle. What was it? The unfinished paper? Susan? Susan was gone. Why the hell hadn't he sat in the back? Kingsfield would get him now, now that the cases had been scared out of him.

The professor silenced the student behind Hart. He leaned over the lectern, focusing on Hart, the center of a ring of tired rejects, each of whom had been singled out and

128

found wanting. Hart's mind filled with the names of those tired students, but he could not recall a single case.

Kingsfield called on Ford, forty seats from Hart.

"Do you think, Mr. Ford," Kingsfield said, "you could explain why the last answer was unsatisfactory?"

"Yes," Hart said, "the last answer." Then he stopped because he could not remember the last answer and bowed his head. When he looked up, he realized Ford was answering the question.

Sometimes things happen in class that you don't expect and are hard to explain. Once one of my professors said to the class: "I want to see Planet of the Apes, *but no one will go with me."*

Everyone talked about it afterward. You see, he just blurted it out while giving a very technical lecture on the parol evidence rule. The class copied down the phrase "planet of the apes" along with citations to cases and laws. I guess we discussed the incident for maybe three weeks at lunch in Harkness. Some people wondered if they should see the movie in case a question about it appeared on the exam.

Much later I sat next to this professor at dinner. After he'd had a couple of drinks, I asked him if he'd ever seen Planet of the Apes.

"Planet of the Apes?" *he said.* "Why would I want to see trash like* Planet of the Apes?"

35

KEVIN LOOKED out over the faces in the classroom. It was hard to tell age. At least half were married. Some had babies. Others had them on the way. He wondered what they did with their wives. Maybe it had been a mistake to get in with Hart and Ford. Maybe he should have gotten into a study group with married students.

Class floated before him like an old movie. He had no idea what case they were on. Last night, trying to work on his outline, he'd fallen asleep over his book and Asheley had taken him to bed.

He looked at the student next to him, searching for the page number of the material being discussed. Down near the front, far off to the right, he saw his empty seat. It looked lonely without him and he felt responsible for it. He wished the seats weren't assigned because it was a good seat and if he wasn't going to use it someone else should have.

Kingsfield looked at the seating chart, picking a name. Kevin knew that it would be his own name. There wasn't any question about it. Kingsfield glanced up, and his eyes met Kevin's. Kevin scrunched down in his seat, hiding in the back.

"Mr. Brooks," Kingsfield said, looking toward the empty assigned seat and then over the entire classroom. "Is Mr. Brooks here today?"

The boys around Kevin smiled. They'd been through it before. They'd had Kingsfield drill into them the fact they lacked the courage to man their seats. Their smiles almost made Kevin rise up and answer. Almost made him call out:

Yes, I'm here, in the back. But he didn't, because people don't do that when they sit in the back.

"Well," Kingsfield said, "I guess Mr. Brooks couldn't come to class today."

Kevin released his grip on the desk top. His mind floated somewhere near the ceiling, careening in weird jagged patterns. He had an image of coming into class with his gun, sitting down in his seat, and when Kingsfield asked him a question, leveling down the gun barrel along a sight that ended in Kingsfield's gold watch.

"Mister, y'all called on the wrong student."

"Mister, I think you better take another look at that there chart of your'n."

And then letting fly, carving up the vest.

36

BELL CAME IN and the circle was complete.

"How come you're not using oil skins anymore?" Hart said, watching Bell take the two huge binders out of his briefcase. Bell had given up trying to wrap his outline in plastic and had replaced it with the sturdy binders, each one holding three hundred of the yellow sheets.

"Funny, very funny," Bell said.

"It's going to cost you a fortune to Xerox that," Hart said, "and I bet the pen won't come out clearly either."

"Maybe I'm not going to Xerox it," Bell snarled.

"What does that mean, maybe you won't Xerox it?" Kevin said.

"I mean, this is a good outline, and if yours don't stack up, maybe you won't get a chance to look at it," Bell snapped.

"Christ," Ford said. "Not today, all right? It's getting too late in the year to argue. Bell's going to have his outline Xeroxed just like the rest of us."

"Maybe Bell is, and maybe Bell isn't," Bell said.

"Personally, I think you're counterproductive," Anderson said. "Bell, you must know that if you refuse to share your outline with us, then we will refuse to share ours with you. You will, thus, only pass one course and flunk out of school."

"I really don't care about any other course except property," Bell said.

"What the fuck kind of thing to say is that," Ford said. "Look, Bell, we've got to get to work and you're making it very difficult."

"I don't care if I flunk the other courses," Bell said. "I have to finish my outline and I don't really have time for any other course except property."

"The outline is a tool, Bell," Anderson said. "A tool, not an end in itself."

"I'm going to publish my outline," Bell said, and his face lit up.

"So, you're going to publish your outline," Ford shot back. "Did it ever occur to you that your outline is merely a summary of a casebook? And that the casebook has already been published?"

"My outline is better than the casebook," Bell said. "Anyway, it's going to be longer."

"God," Ford moaned, "if this goes on for the next two months, we'll all flunk."

"Listen, Bell," Kevin said, and his voice was high-pitched, worried. "We have to stick together. Please don't talk like that."

"I think you're all pimps," Bell said. "If you had any balls, you'd be trying to write an outline as good as mine."

"You're on a suicide course," Anderson said. "You've become, is the correct word schizophrenic?"

"I won't sit here and be insulted," Bell snarled. "One more word out of you, Anderson, and I'll lock your head in your attaché case."

Ford rocked back in his chair.

"All right, we're just going to sit here quietly for the next three minutes. No one is going to say anything. Then after we've all enjoyed the silence, we'll start this meeting over again."

37

Susan's street was quiet, empty and warm in the spring air. Halfway down, she saw a boy in the shadows across the street, sitting on the curb between two parked cars. She slipped off her shoes, crossed, and crept along the sidewalk behind him.

It was Hart, staring up at her window, his feet in the road and his arms around his knees. She sat down quietly beside him, resting her arm on a car fender.

"Do you do this often?" she said softly. "I mean, do you look at my window every night?"

"Don't flatter yourself," he said quickly, in a low whisper, and started to rise. She took his hand.

"Come on," she said, "what the hell is wrong with looking in a girl's window? I like it. It makes me feel good to know you're here, guarding the house. You are guarding the house? I'll sleep better."

"I won't be here long," he said, but he sat down again.

"Look, you won't see anything in my window anyway," Susan said. "On the other hand, over there is a window with all sorts of promise." She pointed to the house next to hers. In the lighted second floor window, he saw the back of a girl's head, poking over a couch.

"It's all bullshit," Susan said, releasing his hand. "That girl up there will tell you, 'I can't love you.' She'll say it all intense, and then go to bed with you. You know, everyone here is messing everyone else up and then saying that it doesn't count. This street is like a swamp. Cambridge is like a swamp."

"I don't know Cambridge the way you do," Hart said.

"It's late," Susan said. "I've been with my father, and I feel like three days have passed. How long has it been since I've seen you? Three months?"

Hart said nothing. She seemed so beautiful. A cloud welled up in his mind, and he shut his eyes for an instant, containing himself, trying not to make a mistake.

"I'm glad," she added. "I don't know. I'm glad you're here."

"I was just walking by," he said.

"Come on, Hart," she said softly. "You weren't just walking by. Goddamn it, I'm glad you were watching my window. This is a special night. It's warm. It's spring. We're sitting here, like two old friends."

A car went by and they ducked down out of the headlight beams. He told himself not to make it more than it was.

Her voice changed and she spoke over-seriously. "This girl you're watching," she said. "Is she really crazy? She double-cross you or something? You planning to take revenge because she left you behind? Maybe you're waiting to rape her when she comes out?"

She put an arm around him and whispered in his ear.

"I hope you get her," she said. "I hope you beat the shit out of her. I know that hussy. She don't listen to nobody.

She throws her ass all around Cambridge." She put her arms around his neck and kissed him slowly, as if she were licking ice cream.

"You just take that hussy and teach her a thing or two," she whispered. "You wait out here long enough and I know she'll come sauntering out, not expecting a damn thing. Then you sneak up and grab her quick-like." She let him go.

"Look," she said, "I'll help you. I'll sit here with you and watch for her. I can distract her while you sneak."

"Jesus," he cried in a long whooshing burst. He turned to her. Felt her hair, running against the side of his face. He buried his head in her shoulder, and wrapped his arms around her back, holding on as hard as he could. He stayed that way for a long time and she did not move.

"This was good," he said finally. "Don't ask me up. It was good just to see you."

"I wasn't going to ask you up," she said.

"I know," he said. He pulled her up with him and watched her walk across the street to her apartment.

38

HART AND FORD stood together at the back of the classroom, under the tall windows, looking down over the descending ribbons of seats. Just in front of the podium, five boys were jockeying for position on the stairs leading up to the lectern. On the top step, a boy in a green plaid jacket refused to yield position to the boy, one step below, who held the present.

"Goddamn," Ford said.

Up on the blackboard someone had written *Happy Birthday, the torts class* in wavy letters made with the side of the chalk.

"Did you ever give any money?" Ford asked.

"No," Hart said, "I never did. Is it because they want a good grade?"

"I don't know," Ford said. "I think they want to purge themselves of their hate. Really. But I guess they have different reasons."

In the next instant the German professor, Vorgan Temby, came through the door. Perhaps he thought it was some kind of protest. He froze and then started backing away.

"What iz ziss . . ." the German stammered. "Iz somezing wrong? Do you want somezing?" He was terrified having them up at the lectern. They'd broken some kind of magic, mental dividing line.

The boy in green reached down, took the present from the boy on the next step and at the same time started to sing, alone, in a squeaky high-pitched voice:

"Happy Birthday, Dear Professor . . ."

The group on the steps joined in. Green coat tried to give the present. The professor backed further toward the door. A bomb? A trick? And then green coat plunked the present down in the professor's arms. He gripped it and shut his eyes, as if he was trying to keep whatever was in the box from popping out. After a few seconds, the professor relaxed. After all, the box hadn't blown up. He was still standing there on the podium, alive. He turned and saw the sign on the blackboard.

"Sank you," the professor said, smiling at his deliverance.

And the class started to applaud.

39

IT WAS THE HEIGHT of the lunch hour rush and the dining room was crowded. Hart would have liked to eat alone but all the tables were full. Reluctantly, he pushed himself between Anderson and Bell. He took the salt from Ford, sitting across the table, and spread it over the thin meat patty on his plate.

"No, I'm not going to go," Anderson was saying. "I don't like parties. They distract me. I'll spend the night in the library."

"Go where?" Hart asked. He tried to cut the patty with his fork but it sprung out of the rubberized meat.

"To Kevin's surprise party," Anderson said.

"For Christ's sake," Hart said, "you can take the night off. Look, his wife planned the whole thing. She's pregnant, you know."

"Kevin couldn't make someone pregnant," Bell muttered.

"I'd like to go," Anderson said. "But I just can't. I've worked out my studying schedule to the end of the year. What's the use of having a schedule if you don't use it?"

"Let's not talk about your studying schedule," Ford said. "Not at lunch."

Hart managed to separate the patty with a knife. He could see the blood vessels running through it. An especially ugly vein was hanging limply across his plate like spaghetti. He put down his fork.

"He's in the study group," Hart said. "That should make you go."

"Who cares about the study group?" Bell said. "What's he ever done for us? Who's ever seen his outline? Look, I bring my outline with me. Have you ever seen Kevin's outline?"

"I don't want to hear about Kevin's outline," Ford said. "And I don't want to hear about your outline. In fact, your outline is the last thing I want to hear about."

Hart looked at Ford. "Don't you think these guys should go to the party?" he said.

Ford had finished eating and his tray was piled with the leftovers, his silverware and napkin. He pushed it to the center of the table.

"I don't know," Ford said quietly. "Kevin makes me nervous."

40

THE PLUSH NEW FACULTY office building, in which Hart stood waiting for the elevator, had none of the monastic feeling of Langdell. There were carpets, bathrooms everywhere and small alcoves designed to relax faculty-student conversations.

Contracts class had ended fifteen minutes before and Hart was tired. He'd done well in class. Perhaps because his mind felt like a festering sore, he had been encouraged to block it out. He had fused with the cases, locked out the world. His answers had been clean.

The elevator doors opened bashfully, coming halfway open, scampering back, and finally jerking forward again in a programmed dance. Hart stepped into the cage and pressed the third floor button. He was going to pick up what was promoted as the last handout in torts, but which would probably be followed by others.

As he leaned against the rear of the car, anticipating the massage he would get as the machine took over and deliv-

ered him upstairs, he began to feel a tingling numbness
— the same feeling he got in class when he was going to be
called on, a warning. He looked quickly around the empty
cage, wishing the doors would shut faster. In the same instant, a hand slammed against the sensitized rubber edges
and the doors sprang back like students.

"Gotcha," Kingsfield said proudly to the retreating doors.
He squinted his eyes for a second and then settled in the
middle of the car. The doors closed, locking the two of them
together.

As the machine began its climb, Hart's neck started to
ache as if a scalding washcloth, draped around his shoulders,
was dripping hot fluid. He tried to reach his arm up and
rub, but his arm would not move.

Kingsfield shifted his weight from one foot to the other.
To Hart, the act seemed to ridicule his own impotency.
Why couldn't he move? It was as though the small confines
of the cage trapped the professor's suffocating presence,
normally dispersed throughout the entire classroom.

Hart tried to pretend he was giving another person advice.
It's all in your mind, he told himself. You're making a big
thing out of nothing. He's just an old man.

But it made no difference. His legs began to weaken,
melt. Hart prayed the elevator would climb faster.

Suddenly, as the car started to decelerate, Hart's body burst
with heat. He looked at Kingsfield's dark suit, striped with
tiny white lines, and he knew it was Friday, because Kingsfield wore this suit on Friday. He knew that tonight he
would have to go to the library and study like a madman,
because the fact that he was in the car would trigger something in Kingsfield's mind. When Kingsfield was searching
for a person to call on an impression of Hart would flicker
in the professor's subconscious.

As the car stopped, and the doors began to jiggle away from each other, the paralyzing vapor dispersed through the opening. The light from the third floor hallway flooded in, reaching past Kingsfield to Hart, and with the light, Hart relaxed, breathed for the first time.

Kingsfield stepped out. Then he turned and caught sight of Hart pressed like a mosaic against the back of the elevator.

"Oh," Kingsfield said, surprised, as if when he'd entered he had somehow missed the fact that Hart was in the car. "You. You did well in class today. Your mind seems to be getting sharper."

Then the elevator doors were shut. The machine started to move down to the first floor, where a student waited for the car to lift him up to the third floor, to the German professor's office and the torts handout. Hart pressed the buttons, trying to stop the elevator, make it reverse course. The buttons did nothing but register the machine's steady decline to the first floor.

Hart gave up and looked around the empty steel shell. Then, in a purging burst, he shoved his feet apart, his hands straight up in the air, and screamed.

41

"BEFORE WE BEGIN the discussion," Ford said, "let's see how things are going. You know what I mean. The outlines."

Anderson smiled.

"I'll start," he said. "I have not yet reached the stage where my outline is reducible to a single word. Yet at fifty pages, if I may pat myself on the back, it is clean and concise."

"All right," Ford said. "Kevin?"

"It's coming," Kevin muttered, turning red.

"Could you tell us how far?"

"Well, I guess I can only say that it will be ready in four weeks, before exams. I haven't had much time lately. I've been trying to catch up in other courses," Kevin said. "I'm really going to work on it."

"That's all right, Kevin," Ford said.

"Wait a minute," Bell said, "I don't think Kevin has an outline. I think the pimp is holding out on us."

"One more word," Ford said slowly. His hand shook: the pencil he was holding vibrated, tapping against the table. "If you ever say pimp in front of me again . . ."

"Pimp," Bell said.

"Kill you," Ford growled.

"You know all you need to know about my outline," Bell shouted. "It's eight hundred pages long and it's fantastic. Figure on this, Ford: Hart is the only one I'm going to let see it."

Hart looked up, astonished.

"He's the only one who isn't a pimp," Bell went on. "I was going to let you see it, Ford, but I've changed my mind. And as far as the robot goes," Bell looked over at Anderson, "I was never going to let him see it."

"Get out," Ford said, standing. "Get the fuck out."

"It's a pleasure," Bell said, "you pimp . . ."

It looked as if Ford would sweep the table up and throw it at Bell.

"Get out," Hart exploded at Bell. "Because so help me God, I'm going to castrate you before Ford kills you — and hang your . . ."

Hart stood up across from Ford, his eyes burning.

Bell began to back toward the door.

"Come on, Hart," Bell said, whimpering. "You don't mean it. YOU AND ME HART, YOU AND ME . . ."

"OUT, OUT," Hart screamed. Bell hit the door with his back, turned and fled.

They sat quietly for a while, avoiding each other's eyes.

"It's quite amusing," Anderson said, breaking the silence. "I wonder if our dropout rate is paralleled in other groups. Two out of six, you know."

"What's going to happen?" Kevin said slowly. "We don't have any outlines in property or civil procedure now. By the end of the year, in a month, when exams come, maybe we won't have any. I need the outlines. I need them. I need help."

"Nothing's going to happen, Kevin," Ford said, his voice tired and irritated. "Take a rest. Go somewhere and rest your mind. We'll meet again next week and figure something out."

"I can't wait," Kevin yelled. "I've got to plan. It's all right for you — you talk in class."

"Kevin," Ford snapped, "we're all in the same boat. Shut up."

"Well," Anderson said, "I'll see you gentlemen next week. Kevin, come with me and we'll get something to eat." He led Kevin out.

Ford pushed back his chair. It slid across the waxed linoleum, skating four feet to the window.

"Shit," Ford said. "Screw O'Connor, Bell and Kevin."

He walked to the chair and looked out the window. The lawn was green and new in the sun. A girl pedaled her bike along the path in front of Langdell, her long blond hair floating out behind her as she accelerated. She must be going over to the college. Law students, standing on the steps of Langdell, watched her go by. Ford rubbed his palms over his eyes.

Then he bent down mechanically, sizing up the wooden law school chair. He put his hands down on its sides and slid it slowly back and forth over the slick floor as if he were dancing with it. With one big swing, he sent it spinning around, screeching across the room. It hit the wall near the door and fell over on its side, breaking two legs. Ford looked up at Hart and smiled.

"Want to eat?" Ford said.

"Sure," Hart said.

"And will you do something for me? I can't do it myself. Go over and take Kevin some notes. Try to get him going on his outline. Try to help the poor bastard."

"Sure," Hart said. "I'll try."

42

KEVIN LAY IN BED, staring at the ceiling. There was no light in the room. Asheley drew the shade when she undressed and didn't like it up until she had her clothes on in the morning.

He inched his hand over and felt her back. It was wet, heated, and he knew she was in deep sleep. He tried to focus on the ceiling to stop his mind from churning. He could get up, go out to the living room and smoke. He twisted, pulling the covers over him.

"Asheley," he said, not really calling her, not daring to wake her. "Asheley," he said louder, forcing away any thought that he was actually waking her, making himself believe he was a machine, just moving with no control. She rolled away, dug her head into the pillow.

He crept into the living room and sat down beside the window, looking out into the dark from the dark. He rested the barrel of his gun on the sill and roamed the sight over the street, sighting on lovers walking in the night.

A white flash hit him. His body became cold, and poured sweat. I'm going crazy, he thought. Maybe I am crazy. I'm sitting at my window, aiming a gun at people: that's what crazy people do.

It made him roll over, double up with laughter. Jesus, he said to himself, I'm crazy. They've screwed up the whole thing, let in some goddamned crazy son of a bitch. Then the laughter turned to tears and he held onto the chair, his head down in it, supporting himself by wrapping his arms around the chair legs. He lay there moaning for a long time. Then his tears dried and his mind began to sweep in long calm rhythms. He got up and turned on a light near the sofa. His outline was on the coffee table and he picked up his pencil and started going over it.

43

HART TURNED THE CORNER and was in the yard in back of Langdell. He glanced absent-mindedly up at the huge stone building and saw the light on in Kingsfield's office. It was five, just beginning to grow dark. He walked further into the yard until, sufficiently far from Langdell, he could see the entire building, spreading out around him like a giant wall. He gazed at the dark stone.

Anderson was standing under a tree near him, looking too. It was curious to see Anderson there, and Hart walked over. Anderson had a pad in his hands, as if he were taking notes in class.

"What's up?" Hart said pleasantly. "Just walking?"

"No," Anderson said. He looked nervously at Hart and tucked his pad under his arm.

"The building really gets to you, doesn't it?" Hart said. "It's almost like an animal. You know, a big animal."

"I'm not watching the building," Anderson said. "It doesn't affect me one way or the other."

Hart looked in the direction Anderson was facing. "Hey, you're looking into Kingsfield's office," Hart said, his mouth rounding in a smile. "You really can see in from back here, can't you." It made him feel close to Anderson.

"I'm not watching him," Anderson said stiffly. "I'm studying him."

"Studying him?" Hart said.

"I want to learn how best to maximize my time, so I use him as a model. It's all related to grade point."

"Grade point?" Hart said.

"That's right. I'm seeing how he organizes his time. It's an experiment. I've thought of asking him about it, but you know, he's awfully busy. Anyway, he might forget something if I asked. He might get something wrong."

"Right," Hart said.

"You know," Anderson said, almost pleadingly, "you can't just go into his office and ask him things like that."

"I know," Hart said.

He stepped away from Anderson, onto the path, and turned to walk away.

"Just grade point," Hart said as a good-bye.

"That's right," Anderson said. "Just grade point."

"Well," Hart said, "good luck."

"Thanks," he heard Anderson say.

44

KEVIN WALKED SLOWLY. He was early, expected at four and it was only quarter of. Kevin had a clean notebook under his arm. He had bought it to hold Moss's prescription for the exam. About fifty yards ahead he saw the house and stopped, taking his time.

Then he saw the girl, the girl from the mixer. She was still far away but walking in his direction. As he watched, she seemed to pick up her pace, and he thought for one horrifying second that she was rushing to catch him. He froze.

In the next instant she had stopped on the sidewalk. She straightened her skirt, walked up the porch steps, and pressed the bell that said Hammer, Moss, and Foswhisher.

The last thing Kevin saw before he fled for home was the beer belly, smiling as he took her inside.

45

FORD LEFT LUNCH early, leaving Hart sitting alone in Harkness dining room, finishing his Jello. Hart turned his chair around, put his feet up on the windowsill. Behind him, people talked, dropped spoons, spilled milk. The cash register went *ping*, *ping*, welcoming people.

He heard snatches of conversations:

"No, I haven't finished my outline . . ."

". . . I hate property."

". . . I was going into the Peace Corps anyway . . ."

". . . that professor knows how to hate . . ."

". . . I love Professor . . ."

His Jello melted in the sun. The dining room became oppressive. Hart walked out, avoiding people, staring at his feet.

He curled under a tree in the yard, letting the sun warm him. He brought his arms under his head for a pillow, pulled his legs to his stomach and lay on his side, his eyes closed.

On the path, students walking to Langdell joked together. Sometimes he could hear the sharp definitive sounds of strong steps. He imagined it was Kingsfield walking along the path and that Kingsfield was watching him, wondering how any student had the time and the nerve to sleep in the yard.

He listened to lovers shuffling down the path — first the sound of one stepping tentatively forward, and then the sound of the other scurrying to catch up. A sound like the syncopated beat of a Slinky going downstairs.

A dog came over and sniffed him and then licked his ears. The dog lay down on the grass and put his head on Hart's leg. If he could not have Susan, he would have this dog. He tried mental telepathy. Said in his mind: Dog, don't leave me. I will stay with you here in the grass in front of the law school and be your pillow for as long as you want me. You and me, dog.

Then the sun wrapped itself in a cloud and it got colder and a little damp. The dog left for other trees and Hart felt lonely. He sat up and rubbed his eyes. His cheeks were wet. He looked at the moisture in his hands, lifted it to his nose and sniffed. Was it the grass, or had he been crying?

When he reached the dorm, he found some students had set up beer cans at the end of the hall and were using them as pins in a bowling game. Hart stood patiently behind the bowlers, waiting for a break in the action. Finally the ball smashed into the beer cans and brought three boys out of their rooms, shouting at the bowlers. Hart stepped into his room.

Gradually, the noise fell away and he locked into his books. He studied through dinner.

At ten, Hart closed his casebook, picked up three of his notebooks and put on his parka. Outside, he fought the pull that tried to take him to Susan's and wandered off toward Kevin's apartment house.

He found Asheley standing on the third floor, looking down over the banister, her stomach bulging out under her dress. Her blond hair glowed in the light coming from the open door but her face was cut with lines and her eyes were swollen. Only her voice still bubbled.

"This is surprising," she said. "Why this is wonderful. You've come to see Kevin. I know he'll be glad."

Real lamps that stood up from the floor lit the living room. There was a real coffee table and real sofas with pillows that matched. It was the kind of room that he could imagine his parents having decorated.

Hart said thank you when Asheley asked if he wanted coffee, and watched her retreat down the hall. Then he sat on the real sofa and waited. Kevin came in with the coffee. He fell backward into the armchair and stared out the window while Asheley arranged the cups.

"This is pretty," Hart said hopefully, pointing to a silver bowl holding cookies.

"My parents gave it to us, for parties," Asheley said, winking. "Now, I'm going to leave you to talk your law school talk. I'd only be in the way."

"I brought you some notes," Hart said to Kevin when Asheley had gone.

"Thanks," Kevin said. "I haven't really been getting what goes on in class." The voice was a low whine. Hart leaned away from the sofa back.

"Good luck studying," Hart said hopefully. "Don't worry, we're all in the same boat." He started to rise.

"No," Kevin said, "we're not all in the same boat." He looked at Hart for the first time. "You and Ford will make Law Review, and the robot too."

"That's crazy," Hart said.

"I mean it, all of you talk in class." Kevin's words trailed off and then he started again, this time more high-pitched. "You and Ford, you've got it made."

"Get some sleep," Hart said. "It's not what you say in class, it's what you write on the exam."

"I started the year wrong," Kevin said. "I wish I could start over. I could do it better. I could do a lot better, if I could start over."

Hart's stomach began to twinge. Kevin would pass. Everyone would.

"You shouldn't be telling me this," Hart said. "You're psyching yourself out. Get some sleep. The study group has been bad."

"I'm sorry," Kevin said. He seemed to be exerting some special kind of energy. The vessels on his neck stuck out from the skin. "We'll work it out. The study group will think of something."

"That's right," Hart said.

"If things go wrong," Kevin asked slowly, "will you help me?"

"Things won't go wrong," Hart said.

"Maybe you'd talk to Kingsfield, if things go wrong. Maybe you can get him to give me another chance."

"Things won't go wrong."

150

"You know him." Kevin's eyes were pleading circles. "You're his favorite. Everyone knows that. He asked you to write a paper."

Hart stood up, his face red. "I don't know Kingsfield. I don't know him."

"I guess I'd say the same thing, if I were you," Kevin said quietly. The room. Asheley. Kevin in the corner. It all built. Hart wanted to run. He wanted to be out in the street, running as fast as he could go. Then he softened, as he realized he wouldn't be able to run.

"Sure, Kevin," Hart said. "If anything goes wrong, I'll talk to Kingsfield. Don't worry. He's a good guy. He likes you. He thinks you're doing a good job."

Asheley walked him to the landing. When they were alone and Hart had taken a step down the stairs, she touched his shoulder.

"Don't bring a present," she said. "That's not important."

He tried to understand what she meant, and then he remembered the party.

"Sure," he said, "I won't bring a present."

"We'll be looking for you," she whispered, as he started down the stairs. "It's going to help Kevin to see all his friends."

46

AROUND THE MAIN DESK of the library several boys, abandoning all discretion, flirted openly with the girls who handed out books. It made Hart think of Susan, and torts became even more repulsive. He pushed the blue book aside and leaned back in his chair. He'd use Ford's outline — he'd pass somehow — but he just couldn't look at another case.

Across the table, Ford was bent over his work. Why disturb him? Someone had to study torts. Hart left, walking fast, conscious that bored students were watching him, knowing that the fact he was leaving was another piece of data in their decisions: I beat him. I studied longer. Well, I don't have to worry about Hart. He can't even stay in the library after eleven.

Hart paused on the ground floor of Langdell. The hall was lonely without students pushing through the classroom doors. Almost ghostly. He walked to the door of the contracts classroom. Even late at night and alone, he could not approach this opening casually. It was just a mute piece of architecture, old and unguarded, but somehow it conveyed a special allegiance to Kingsfield. He knew no one was inside. Yet when he walked toward the door, he shivered. It didn't seem fair: Why should it hurt him? What had he done? He walked into the contracts classroom.

As his eyes adjusted to the darkness on the other side of the door, he made out the stars and the moon, shimmering in the tall thin windows that lined both sides of the hall. The stars seemed to be held in the glass, as if they were an integral part of the design, not distant points. Against the night, the windows were like stained glass — dark blue sprinkled with tiny white candles.

He saw the benches, falling in rows to the center, decreasing in half circles, leading down to the front. Finally, sprouting from the black pit below, he saw the lectern itself, the dark center of it all, Kingsfield's special territory, rising above the stage.

There was movement outside the hall, the sound of students leaving the library. Hart ducked below the window until the outer door slammed and he knew they were gone.

Why was he worried? Someone looking in would see only black. He turned again toward the lectern. Behind it, on the far wall, the faces of the judges peered at him from their gilt frames. He could not see their dark robes. But the starlight shining off the white tones made the faces parched and three-dimensional, like old relics in a shrine, glistening skulls. They looked reproachful, as if he was violating them by coming before the morning. What the hell was the matter with them? Why did they look up at him that way? He was related to the room too — it didn't belong solely to the old judges and Kingsfield. After all, he was almost the living extension of the old judges. He carried in his mind the cases they had written. Where the hell would the judges be without him? Who would hang their pictures if there were no law students? It was hard being the living extension of tradition. Hart wondered if the judges had ever considered his difficulties when they wrote the cases that now were printed in his casebooks.

He walked the center aisle until he stood in the pit between the first seats and the lectern. He reached up into the darkness and touched the lectern's smooth wooden side. He crept up the side stairs and stepped onto the stage.

He was standing in Kingsfield's place. He gripped the stand, expecting some kind of special force, some magical charge, to whip through his fingers and repel them. All he felt was the old wood and the grooves worn by Kingsfield's fingers. Could that be all, he thought? Could anyone come and stand here? He wished the lectern could talk. God, it must know the secrets of Kingsfield. He could not believe that the wood was inanimate. It must help Kingsfield. There must be secret buttons hidden in it. Did Kingsfield feel nothing more than this when he stood here?

His hearing had increased — the tiniest noise rebounded

to him, coming to rest at the lectern. He heard a shade swing softly against a window top and the faint whirr of the electric clock. He looked out over the black classroom. Where was his seat? How far to the left? How many spaces between his seat and the wall? He could not find it. His sense of direction was thrown off by the unfamiliar vantage point.

The classroom looked almost sinister. Because of the darkness, Hart wondered? The curving benches, spreading out below him, seemed like the ribs of some sleeping beast, immense and forbidding, lying at his feet but ready to spring up — a serpentlike animal, coiled in faint red circles. He smiled, thinking the red was merely the bench tops, but the smile was forced and hollow.

He felt an overwhelming desire to say or do something. Why the hell should only Kingsfield and the old judges leave their marks on this room? He wanted to shout. What if the beast heard him and awoke? What if it tried to encircle his high point and devour him? He felt confident — from his perch, he could guard and watch all sides, throw down the mountain anything the beast might set against him. Instinctively, Hart looked quickly to his right and left, to the stairs that led down toward the beast's resting place. He gripped the lectern harder, forcing his fingers into the grooves. The lectern was strong and steady: a perfect breastplate to hold back the curving serpent.

A sound interrupted him. The light flowing from the tiny window in the door blinked out and then on. Had the beast wakened? Was this the first onslaught? Or was it Kingsfield, come to ferret him out of the throne? He tried to bring himself back to reality. He was merely standing in a classroom. There was no beast. Kingsfield was home in bed. He was just standing at the lectern of a dark classroom and in a few minutes he would leave and walk back to the dorm.

Another sound ricocheted off the walls and reflected to the lectern. Someone was in the hall. Something was in the lecture hall with him. Someone, Hart told himself. He looked at the curving ribs of the beast. Benches, he said to himself.

And then the classroom was filled with light. For an instant it blinded him and he fell back, toward Kingsfield's small door, whirling in the light, losing direction. In the next minute his eyes had cleared. He saw the classroom: papers lying in the aisles waiting for the janitor to come in the morning and sweep, in the corner a contracts book forgotten, and behind him, merely the dull dusty blackboard and the paintings.

At the back of the room, standing at the light switch, was Ford.

Hart jumped from the stage and ran back to him.

"Jesus," Ford called to him as he ran, "you're white as hell."

"I know," Hart panted. "You took me by surprise."

47

It was after ten and though it was Saturday night, the night of Kevin's party, the dorm was alive with the sound of typewriters and students pacing. Throbbing with the beginnings of a paranoid attempt to catch up and master all the material that had slipped by.

Hart threw his books down on his desk and looked at his watch. It was ten-thirty. The party was sure to be at least half over. Reluctantly he put on a sweater, looked once in the mirror, checked to see if his wallet was in his hip pocket, and went to Ford's room.

Ford was lying on his bed.

"Goddamn it," Hart said, flicking on the light switch. "It's ten-thirty. Let's go."

Ford groaned and buried his head in his pillow.

"Let's go," Hart said again. "We've already missed most of it."

"I'm not going," Ford said into the pillow.

"Oh yes you are," Hart said. He pulled the pillow from under Ford's head.

"No," Ford said. "No one is going."

"I took him the notes," Hart shouted. "You can go to the party with me."

"I can't," Ford said. "I've tried to do things for Kevin. He screws up my mind. I'd go if other people were going. Don't you understand, I've got to keep my head together."

"Some lonely fucker will show up," Hart said. "Someone always goes to parties. Other people will be there."

"No," Ford said slowly. "No one is going to go."

"Come on," Hart pleaded.

But Ford didn't move.

Kevin closed the bedroom door. He knew the party wasn't just for the two of them. He knew that Asheley had planned for a lot of people. He could tell by the candies lying in the silver bowls. By the Coke and the decorations.

He was in a trance, not realizing how he moved, how his body connected with his thoughts. His knees hit the bed and he sat. He couldn't go back out and he knew he should. He knew he should drink some wine with Asheley and pretend that everything was all right, and he couldn't.

He couldn't tell Asheley about the classroom, and the casebooks, and the study group. He couldn't tell her about the mixer, and Moss, and the girl. About flunking his practice exams, and not having an outline. Asheley didn't understand those things.

It's just a game, he told himself, and went to the closet and got the rifle. He laid it on the bed and opened the bureau drawer. Stuffed into a sock he found the shells. He took them out and rerolled the socks.

He heard Asheley in the kitchen. That would be the cake. She would be lighting the candles. She'd come smiling. Bring the cake right into the bedroom to cheer him up. Instinctively, he backed toward the window, away from the door.

Jesus, Jesus. It was all a game.

From the window, he saw couples walking hand in hand. Car lights, lovers, trees. And far out, to the right, just the top of Langdell. The view seemed to have a power of its own. It knocked him back from the window, toward the door. He fell, leaned against the bureau, and extended both his arms. He held the gun at arm's length so that the barrel pointed at him, so that the tip rested on his forehead.

The kitchen door vibrated. Asheley was backing through it and shielding the cake. He closed his eyes.

And then Hart's running. He's running just to move. He's running like he was back in high school, in a long easy lope, skimming along, looking out ahead, planning each step in advance, jumping in and out of the shadows that the moon lays down from the top of Langdell.

The rain has left the paths coated, and they reflect the light. It looks as though the paths have ice on them, as if he's an ice skater, sliding along beside the big stone building.

He cuts through the faculty driveway, runs along beside the steel fence with points on it, and beyond he sees the buildings, lights on even though it's late, and a law student in each window. But Langdell is dark: stretching up over all the other buildings, a black block, holding up the moon.

It gets easier each step he takes. He has that first wind and he runs like a touring car on a mountain road. He sees people every now and then. Old ladies pretending they're looking into the dark store windows but really trying to melt into the storefronts because they're scared, seeing a boy running this way in the night.

He's run to the end of the side streets and onto the avenue. There's traffic but he doesn't slow down. He leaves the sidewalks, gives up trying to slip through the groups of high school students walking three abreast. He doesn't slow down. He goes right into the middle of the street, dodging the cars. They honk at him. They screech to a stop and let him pass. Car windows are rolled down and he hears screams: "Motherfucker, get out of the road."

He's back in the side streets, along the sidewalks and the parked cars, under the trees that dip down from the little yards. Up ahead, he sees Kevin's apartment building, looking larger than it is against the small frame houses. He pants up to the door, and stops, breathing hard, getting control of himself. And then he rings the bell.

Just when he's about to ring again, the buzzer comes alive, and he throws the door open and starts to climb the stairs.

Asheley stood in the door. Hart stopped four feet away and leaned against the banister. It was absolutely quiet: just the two of them staring at each other on the top of the stairs.

"I guess I missed the surprise," Hart said.

"There isn't any party." Her voice came low and soft, a fog floating around him.

"Could I just say hello to Kevin?" he said. "I'd like to wish him happy birthday." He began to move toward her, trying to smile.

"I don't think it would be a good idea," Asheley said. "Kevin's not feeling well."

"Is it the flu? Everyone gets the flu," Hart said.

"It's not the flu," she said.

He heard a moan. It trickled out around Asheley from the apartment beyond. A low whining gurgle coming from the very bottom of the throat.

She turned and Hart knew she was going to shut the door. She backed through it, rocked against it, so that when the door closed her weight would fall on it. A woman in a trance. Then the groan came again and she hesitated.

Hart pushed through the open space. Ribbons hung from the center of the room. On the coffee table the little silver bowls were filled with bright candies, untouched. A record hung from the spindle, waiting to be pushed down.

Hart walked through the ribbons and into the hall. He heard hard breathing and followed the sound to the bedroom.

He saw a photograph of Asheley and a set of brushes on the bureau. His eyes moved to the bed, rumpled and empty. Then he saw Kevin lying on the floor, his arms thrown over his head and his legs spread apart. Blood oozed from the corners of Kevin's mouth, trickling down his cheek into the rug.

"Leave him alone," Asheley said from the door. Her voice was like compressed air, corked and ready to explode.

"Leave him alone," she said again, this time a little higher, a little more shrill. Hart took a step away from Kevin. He couldn't leave. He wavered back and forth in the middle of the room, with Kevin at his feet.

"He tried to kill himself. I stopped it. I had to. I'm having a baby and he tried to kill himself," she said. "I didn't hurt him. He'll be all right."

She walked slowly across the room to the other side of the bed. Her stomach bulged as she bent down but the action was graceful and slow. When she straightened, she was holding a rifle. Hart watched silently. She leaned the rifle in against her belly, the barrel pointing up, slipped the bolt back with a dull thud, and then slammed it forward. A shell popped over her arm and fell on the bed.

"You would have done the same thing," she said. "I had to and I did it. I'm going to have a baby." She dropped the rifle. It bounced on the bed, coming to rest quietly on the pillow.

"Take it. I don't want it in the house."

"I can't," Hart said.

"Please. Take it and leave."

He picked the rifle up. He didn't know how to hold it and tucked it under his arm like a casebook.

"I'm sorry," he said.

"There isn't anything to be sorry about," she answered quietly. "Thanks for coming. You were the only one who did."

48

HART AVOIDED all the major streets. He kept the gun close to his body, running down the inside of his arm. The barrel stuck out below his hand and he thought the people he passed would call the police.

He walked to Susan's.

She opened the door for him, wearing a long brown dress

gathered at the neck in a yoke. He stumbled past her, tripped on the rug, and collapsed on the couch.

Later, she put him in the car, put the seat back so it formed a kind of bed. He couldn't see anything lying that way and gradually the swaying of the car rocked him to sleep.

He was in front of the fire, wrapped in two blankets, listening to the waves.

"This was my grandmother's house," Susan said. "She only came here for a weekend a year, and it got ruined. There are flagstones under the grass."

He slid down into the blankets and closed his eyes.

"It's fantastic," he said quietly.

"Upstairs, in my grandmother's old room, the windows wrap around three sides and you can look along the beach. We used to own the house on the right, but we sold it after she died."

"The grandmother?" he said.

"Yes. She kept this house to remind her of her husband, but she wouldn't sleep in the bed. Remember? The room with windows on three sides? That was their bedroom and she wouldn't sleep in it after he died because it made her sad."

She pushed the blanket down between the sofa and his body so that it hugged him.

"Thank you," he murmured.

"I'm going to sleep," she said.

"Are you going to sleep in the room with windows on three sides?"

"Why?"

"I don't know. I just wondered."

"Well, I am."

He heard her walking away.

"Susan, this is really nice of you. I needed this."

"I could tell."

"Susan?"

"What?"

"I don't want you to think this is going to start me back trying to organize us."

"It's five. It'll be light soon. Go to sleep. You look like hell."

He heard the door close. The fire sputtered and he fell asleep.

He woke and found her sitting in front of him. Light streamed in the windows. He saw the rug was blue and there was a blue sky outside.

"Do you feel like breakfast?" she asked.

"I'll make it," he said. "Really, don't make it."

"It's made," she said. It was on a tray beside her.

He took her hand and cradled it under him, not wanting her to move. She let him hold it for a minute and then pulled away.

She came back around the front of the sofa, holding the rifle.

"Let's eat on the porch," she said, picking up the tray in one hand and cradling the rifle in the other.

49

O'CONNOR DRONED on and on. He seemed to think that *Springstead* v. *Nees* held the secret of consideration. It wasn't that O'Connor was saying anything silly. In fact he was making a pretty good analysis. But he'd lost track of time and the importance of finishing a certain number of cases today so that they wouldn't have to do them tomorrow. And he didn't seem to realize that Kingsfield was not in a good mood.

Ford fiddled with his pencil and looked at Hart's empty assigned seat. Hart had been the first student Kingsfield had called on during the hour. And the fact that Hart was absent seemed to have disturbed the professor. Ford wondered if he should have said something. Perhaps told Kingsfield that Hart was in the hospital.

Kingsfield looked down at O'Connor and the class tensed, moved back into their seats, anticipating the push that was going to surge from the lectern. Then Kingsfield checked the seating chart and the class wavered because they didn't understand.

"Mr. Bell," Kingsfield said. "What do you think of Mr. O'Connor's argument?"

Bell looked up. "What?" he said. "I think what?"

"I asked you what you thought of O'Connor's argument," Kingsfield said. "Haven't you been listening?"

O'Connor braced.

Bell stumbled. He had been thinking about property and had not heard O'Connor's argument.

"I didn't ask you for an analysis, Mr. Bell. I just want you to say if you found Mr. O'Connor's argument convincing."

The words released Bell. "I don't find anything Mr. O'Connor says convincing," Bell said.

There was suppressed laughter from the class. It was the first time someone, other than Kingsfield, had consciously insulted a student during a class period. The class was unsure how to react and waited for guidance.

"Mr. O'Connor," Kingsfield said. "I don't think everyone is impressed by the importance of what you're saying."

50

THE PORCH was made of heavy flagstones, set in sand, and surrounded by a rock wall that stretched out from the side of the house in a half-circle. They looked down through the brown trees into a blanket of marsh grass and two hundred yards further on, to the beach and the ocean.

Susan was sitting on the wall, her legs dangling over the far side. She faced the beach, the rifle resting across her lap.

"I guess I'm always a little amazed when law students have a hard time," she said, twisting so she could see Hart in the deck chair behind her. "When you grow up with it, you get immune. It's like I don't see Dad anymore. I know he's walking around. I know when I'm with him, but I don't feel him."

"I don't know," Hart said. He closed his eyes. "I sit in that damn class. For days I sit there. Then I read his books in the library, and I abstract the cases he's chosen. I know everything about him. The stripe of his ties. How many suits he has. He's like the air or the wind. He's everywhere. You can say you don't care, but he's there anyway, pounding his mind into mine. He screws around with my life."

"There's just no way you're ever going to have a normal relationship with him. You accept that, and you try to do things on your own," Susan said.

"I don't know," Hart said. She had raised the gun so the butt rested on the wall. "Like our outlines. Every one of his words copied down. Look, I sit in the damned dining hall. What do I hear? I hear people telling Kingsfield stories, about how Kingsfield flattened a particular student in a particular way. It's like they were telling Norse sagas. It's like we were studying theology instead of law. He's arranged it that way. He's everywhere."

"You know," she said, "some people would think you're strange." She laughed. "But as it happens, I agree with you. Of course, my circumstances are special. But that's not the thing. The question is what the hell are you going to do. You've got to stand up. You've got to grow."

She sighted the rifle down the beach. A cold wind blew in from the sea and rustled the trees.

"I can't explain it," she said. "But you've got to stop being so soft."

She fired off two shots, one after the other. He saw the sand fly six inches from a rock and then, with the second report, the rock pitched out of the sand. He sat up.

"Relax," she said. "There aren't any more bullets." She swung around so her legs were on the side of the wall facing the house and put the rifle down.

"Listen," she said, "I'm tired of hearing about my father and tired of talking about him. What about you? Can't you do things? Do you like to sit in class and take shit? Why don't you just tell him you're not in the mood?"

"You don't understand," he said. "The class is like a team. Everyone has to answer questions."

"Jesus," she said, walking over to the chair. She put her hands around his neck and smiled. Then she slapped him hard across the face. He grabbed her arms tightly, holding them to her sides.

"Don't be mad," she said. "I just have to make sure you're alive."

51

FORD WAS WAITING for Anderson on the steps outside Langdell.

"I suppose you've figured out something, now that the study group doesn't have any outlines. O'Connor and Bell are lost and I have a feeling Kevin isn't going to make it," Ford said.

"Of course," Anderson said. "I prepared for this a long time ago. I saw it coming."

A dog scampered up to them and Anderson pulled his attaché case out of harm's way.

"In fact," Anderson said, "I made concise outlines of all courses. It was a lot of extra work."

"You wouldn't want to share them with Hart and me?" Ford said.

"Look, Ford," Anderson said, "I like you. I really do. You were nice to get me into the group and all that, even if it didn't work out well. I'm willing to give you the outline I promised, but not all the extra outlines. It wouldn't help my chances. You might do better than me."

"Thanks," Ford said. "Thanks for everything."

"You haven't seen Hart," Anderson asked, as if nothing had come between them.

"No," Ford said.

"I've been looking everywhere for him," Anderson said.

"Why?"

"Well, it's just sort of business," Anderson said.

"Listen, Anderson," Ford said, "I'm Hart's agent while he's out of town. Anything you have to tell him, you can tell me."

"I don't know," Anderson said, drawing his eyebrows together. "This is really just for Hart."

"You can only get to him through me," Ford said sternly. Anderson hesitated. "All right," he said at last. "You know Hart is the best student in contracts. No, I don't mean best. He's out of anyone else's class in that one course. He's fantastic. I just wanted to make sure I got his outline."

"That's too bad," Ford said carefully. "You see, now that the study group's gone, it's everyone for himself. I'll personally see you get Hart's outline. I'll Xerox it myself for you, but only for two copies of all your outlines. Don't worry, I'll pay for that too."

"I had hoped to talk to Hart," Anderson said. "But I suppose this will have to do."

52

THEY WALKED down the path to the beach barefoot. The sun streamed in over the water, making it look warmer than it was.

"In a month, the ferry will be going by every couple of hours, full of future law students. Some day I'm going to blow up the ferry," Susan said.

"Why?" he said.

"It makes too much noise," she answered. They stopped ten yards from the waves and watched a sail miles out. Hart didn't want to go back and face exams and the dorms. He wanted to stay with her. It was like a dream.

"I'm not looking forward to going back to class with your father," he said.

"I'm not particularly interested in seeing him either. I wish there was more of a family. It would have been better to have brothers and sisters," she said.

"I'll be your brother," Hart answered, smiling. "You can start growing up all over again. You were too young to go to college anyway. We can live here while you grow up."

"All right," she said. "You can be my brother."

She pulled her arms into her sides, rocked around on her left foot, dug into the sand, and then lunged back with her fist. It came in over his shoulder, and caught him on his cheek, sent his head snapping down toward his shoulder.

"You're crazy," he said, backing away. "You're really crazy."

"Sibling rivalry," she said, smiling. "Did you know it hurts more to be hit on the side of the head, because the head can't rock back and absorb the impact?"

"Watch it," Hart said. She was dancing toward him. "I don't want to hurt you."

"Come off it. I could wipe you out," she said, moving to his side. "Hart, you're so full of illusions, you can't do anything human. Your brain is all confused. You can't hit a woman, can you?"

Her arm flicked up, diverting his eyes, and then with the other arm she jabbed her hand into his belly, her fingers straight so that the hand sank in like a knife. He doubled up, fell to his knees.

"You see, Hart," she snapped, "I don't even have to try to mash you. You can't hit back and you're not agile enough to avoid me. You're bound to lose. Just like the law school, isn't it?"

His breath came back and he got up on one knee. Then he charged toward her, digging hard into the sand, flying. In the last second, he checked. She looked so soft and small. He slowed to hit her with less power.

She sidestepped as he came, his momentum carried him past her, and she hit down with her fist on his exposed neck.

For an instant, it severed all his nerve connections. He flew on, landing in a heap in the sand.

"I want to return my brother for a newer model," she laughed. "You're just like Kevin, only it's going to take you a little longer to cave in. Maybe you'll wait until you're forty. They should never have let you into class with Dad. He doesn't even have to try. You're like the robots. The law school got you without trying."

He was motionless, throbbing with pain, his eyes half closed.

"You're all right, aren't you?" she asked, looking down.

Then he moved: snapped out his arm like a casting rod and caught her foot, yanked it forward with all his energy, trying to pull the leg out of the socket. She sprawled on the sand in front of him, started to flip over on her side, roll. He shot out his fist. It caught her on the cheek and his knuckles capped with sand scraped down like files, carving four red channels on the side of her face.

She rolled outside his reach, dripping blood.

"You see, you can do things, if you try," she screamed. "You've just got to get angry enough."

They lay for a minute, lying in the molds they'd made in the sand. Finally, she stumbled to her feet. Then she took his hand and pulled him up.

53

"Here's your copy of Hart's contracts outline," Ford said, pushing the neat pile of paper across the table to Anderson. "Let's have your outlines. I'll Xerox them and have them back by the afternoon."

Anderson reached for Hart's outline. He thumbed through it quickly.

"It's good," Anderson said. "I can almost feel it through the paper. This is a good outline."

"The best," Ford said. "No one knows contracts like Hart. Let's have your outlines."

Reluctantly, Anderson opened his attaché case and pulled out five neatly typed outlines. He pushed them across the table to Ford.

"Don't lose them," Anderson said. He sighed. "Please don't lose them."

"Don't worry," Ford said. He stacked the outlines and started to rise.

"One more thing," Anderson said. "You might as well make Kevin a copy. He can't possibly do well enough to upset things. I feel sorry for him."

"Kevin doesn't need a copy," Ford said. "He's left school."

"Christ," Anderson said, "I wish I'd known. I should have said good-bye."

Ford pulled out a brown manila envelope, blew in it to puff it out and then turned it upside down. Three crinkled dirty pages slid onto the table.

"It's Kevin's outline," Ford said. "He'd only done three pages. I got it in the mail yesterday. Maybe you can get some extra insight from it." He started for the door.

"Listen, I didn't do anything," Anderson called after him. "It was Bell who hated Kevin. I never said anything against him."

"I know," Ford said from the door, "I never said you did."

54

THE CLASSROOM WAS HOT. The air hung like flypaper, a premonition of summer. Pages ripped from the students' notebooks as the sweat from hot hands seeped like glue into the paper.

Hart tried to make his mind bend into the cases, but instead it swung along in the hot air currents, and he had fleeting images of Susan, the Cape, Kevin. All the images sliding over each other as if they were suspended in water.

He really didn't have to think in class. Kingsfield was providing a summary of the course and the only important thing was copying it down. In the week that had passed since Hart had come back from the Cape, Kingsfield had referred to constitutional contracts, marriage contracts, historical contracts, French contracts, African tribal contracts, religious contracts and to other subjects which Hart had listed in his notebook but could not bring as easily to mind.

It didn't matter what his answer to a question was. The answers which Kingsfield sought were implied in his questions. They served only to keep the class on its toes, to make certain that everyone would be at least partially prepared for the exam.

The professor slammed the lectern, emphasizing a point. The wooden stand drummed out a sound like a tribal call. Then, without looking at the seating chart, Kingsfield called on Hart.

"Mr. Hart," he said, "will you relate the next case to the summary we've been building?"

It shocked him. He had had no warning. He had thought that Kingsfield wanted, in the closing spasm of the course, to call on those students who might need a special push.

Hart looked at his book, flipped a page, bringing the next case into view. He looked at his small summary typed on tissue paper and pasted into the book. Yes, he could recite this case to the class. He looked back toward the stage. Kingsfield was standing to the side of the lectern, his hands on his hips, pulling his jacket off his chest and thus allowing some breeze to circulate. Kingsfield was waiting.

"I think I'll pass," Hart said quietly.

It was done. He had actually refused to answer a question. The first part was the hardest.

"Pass?" Kingsfield said. "Pass what? Pass the course?"

The dialogue snapped the class from their notes. Rubbing tired hands, they looked first at Hart, and then at Kingsfield, not understanding. Was Hart making a joke? There was laughter. And then the class began to take up their pens again, ready to catch Hart's answer and Kingsfield's summary.

He'd been given a chance to back out. He could answer the question and it would be left at that. The craggy face of the old professor, drawn in fierce lines, seemed to recommend that course. A few students glanced nervously at Hart, as if to say: Don't upset us, don't make a mistake.

"I don't have anything important to say about the case," Hart said. "I'll raise my hand when I do."

Immediately, hands went up around the classroom. Sweaty hot arms were thrown up as students saw in Hart's refusal the chance to prove themselves before Kingsfield. Hart didn't have anything to say. Hart didn't understand the question. Hart, one of the best students in contracts. Hands raised in an attempt to justify the bodies that supported them. Thirty hands raised by thirty students who wanted Kingsfield to give them the chance to shoot Hart down.

"You don't have anything to say?" Kingsfield said, for an instant puzzled. He looked at the seating chart, as if to make certain it was Hart talking. The hands of the class stretched up higher. Seats of pants inches off seats of chairs. Students wanting to bust Hart up and prove themselves.

The professor took out his handkerchief and mopped his brow. It was entirely appropriate. The room was stifling and there was sweat on his forehead. But Hart knew that Kingsfield was crafty, that he was mopping his brow to gain a few seconds in which to think.

Then Kingsfield laughed. A quick, cutting laugh like ice falling into a glass.

"All right," he said, gripping the lectern with one hand, "I'll tell the class the significance of the case myself." And he did.

Gradually the hands dropped to the desk. The faces belonging to the hands looked disturbed, angry. Somehow Hart had escaped. By all rights, he should have been shot, dragged before the class, his insolence broken. It had happened to others, it should have happened to Hart.

When the session ended and Hart had gathered his books together and walked to the aisle, the student ahead of him, a large, well-dressed, ugly boy with red hair, sneered, "You were lucky, smart ass, he should have let you have it. I guess he felt sorry for you." And then the boy pushed Hart, a smashing blow that caught his shoulder and knocked him back against the students behind.

55

IT WAS THE LAST DAY of class. Down in front, Kingsfield pirouetted, gesticulated, moving the class through its final spasm. They were on the last case. It was very special that months after they'd started, Kingsfield would end on the last page in the book. How many other professors could so exactly delineate the subject, and so completely dominate the class, that no small measure of the students' independent interest would vary the progress?

As Kingsfield's arm cut a wide swath of air, emphasizing a point, the gold watch chain tingled across his vest and the neat row of buttons lifted with his heartbeat.

Hart put down his pen. In five minutes it would be over. Just exams. And what were exams? The dorm was going crazy, but Hart had not started his review. Law school ended for him in this room.

The professor brought his hands together, tying an argument in a knot. Then he shoved his hands out, palms to the class, as he illustrated the universality of another theme.

As the hands of the classroom clock drifted to the hour mark, Hart's eyes began to water. Don't be an ass, he said to himself.

And then Kingsfield threw his head back and shut his book. His hand came down hard on the lectern, booming the sound back and forth across the curving benches. The class had ended.

Hart could not believe it. He had expected some final speech, some last thoughts with which they would wrap themselves in the years ahead. Watching the old professor shuffle his papers together and then tuck his notes and book under his arm, Hart's insides ached with a lonely jabbing pain.

Kingsfield turned and stepped toward the door. The class broke into applause. The noise thundered through the hall, rocking the windows. Slowly, as one body, they rose, each one clapping his hands red.

174

Kingsfield turned back halfway to the door. He looked annoyed at the uncontrolled faces. He shook his head slightly as if to shrug off their gesture.

Then he was gone. They kept clapping for a long time, standing up behind their seats, facing forward toward the stage, clapping as if, like Tinker Bell, Kingsfield would die without them.

56

FORD HAD TO GET OUT. Walking downstairs to get a cup of coffee had become an adventure into the surreal. If you met a friend on the stairs, he'd ask you the name of a case. If you couldn't bring the case to mind, you'd get a silly smile that said: "Hah, you don't know the material. I do. I'm going to do better than you. You will flunk. FLUNK."

Ford knew his limits. He knew that soon he would yield to temptation and start cramming as many facts into his mind as he could. Then he'd look for ways to trap his friends into believing they were stupid.

No one asked about the theories they'd learned. It was always:

"Can you give the facts of . . ."

"Can you tell me the page number of . . ."

Ford knew it was suicide, knew that the dorm was committing mass suicide on the altar of detail.

Hart was dubious, but he started with Ford to a hotel about a mile from the law school. As they were going out the doors of the dorm, each carrying a suitcase filled with notebooks, outlines and casebooks, they met Bell.

He looked completely mad. His eyes had turned round, twitching, and his usually neat hair fell down over his eyes. His gigantic frame blocked the door.

"Where the hell are you going?" Bell yelled.

"We're leaving," Ford said. "Where is none of your business."

"You won't pass," Bell shouted. "You won't pass without my outline."

"O.K.," Ford said. "Then we won't pass."

Ford started to move around Bell, keeping the suitcase in front of him as a shield. With his hand, he signaled Hart to follow.

"I tell you, you can't pass without my outline," Bell screamed.

And then they were past him. Bell watched them walking away down the path.

"I'll let you see it," Bell called. "Really, you can see it. Please, I'll show it to you."

As soon as they got into their room at the hotel, Ford had the television taken out. It was hard to do, but he faced down the big eye and tossed it out.

They paid fifteen dollars a day just for the room, and having the food brought in cost another fifteen. But they were probably the only people getting their money's worth. They never left the room. The only people they saw during the week were the maids who came in around eleven to make the beds. After three days, even that was a distraction and they didn't open the door for them.

That brought the manager up, trying to find out if they'd turned on the gas, or were using the hotel for a homosexual orgy. He saw the books strewn over the floor, the reams of paper spread on the bureau and chairs.

He screamed.

Hart and Ford were sitting on the floor in their underwear and hadn't shaved since they came. The manager said they were putting cigarette butts out on the rug, which they weren't. He threatened to call the police.

Ford unkinked his knees and stood up, glaring.

"If you kick us out of here, you'll ruin our whole goddamned lives. Everything is riding on these seven days. Everything in the world. If we leave now, we'll flunk. We'll lose everything we've worked for." He stared at the manager like a torch. "You kick us out of here and I'll sue your goddamned hotel for a million dollars. I'll burn the fucking place to the ground."

Ford was in a delirium. Hart could see that. He moved in between them. Hart told the manager he'd report the hotel to the newspapers. Tell them they were a dope ring working out of the hotel. He said no one would ever stay there again. Hart looked the manager straight in the eyes and told him to shut up and get out.

The manager flapped down the hall, sputtering to himself, but he didn't come back.

They couldn't get room service that night and their water was cut off. They put through a call to the manager's office and left a message with his secretary. The message said a shipment of dope had come through and they were holding the manager's special brand. The water and room service came back in half an hour.

They pared down the outlines so that almost all the cases were eliminated, leaving just the general theories. Then they memorized the outlines, throwing in the name of a case wherever they thought it might impress a professor. By the end of four days they could recite the outlines of each of the six main courses perfectly.

They practiced running through the outlines while one timed the other. The idea was to repeat the outlines after writing each exam question to make sure they'd left nothing out.

The exams would be four hours long. They took some old exams and practiced, timing themselves.

Then the seven days were up. They came out into the sunshine like prisoners set free. They hadn't seen a newspaper or received any mail. But nothing had happened. Absolutely nothing.

They avoided everyone in the dorms. They didn't say hello, smile, or meet stares. They wanted to remain uncontaminated. They shaved, showered, dressed and then went to a small restaurant near the law school.

There was only minimal conversation over breakfast. In half an hour exams would start and they would be in competition. After breakfast they left each other, wanting in the last minutes to be alone.

It was drizzling, the warm beginning of a summer rain.

Hart stood outside Ames Hall. The exam would begin in ten minutes. He kept away from the small groups of students nervously talking on the lawn. He kept a tree between himself and the others.

He was talking to himself, not openly, but in his mind, addressing himself in commands.

"Listen, Hart," he said, "shake contracts. Pour it out on that exam. Shake it loose and pour it all out. Don't leave the smallest fact in your mind. Make a clean sweep. Write it all down and sweep it out."

At five of nine, he walked into the building, up the steps, taking them one at a time in measured strides, looking straight ahead. Into the building, down the hall, on the last walk.

The exam books were laid out on the desks, an empty seat between each book so that there would be no cheating. Hart took a seat at the side of the room so that there would be as few people around him as possible.

Others were filing in too. Some were studying their outlines in a futile attempt to cram in the things they should have learned before. Others were just moving blindly toward the nearest seat in a short mindless dance, their arms hanging limp at their sides.

"O.K., baby, O.K.," Hart said, rubbing his palms together. The people near him yanked around.

"O.K.," he repeated, "bring that fucking test in here."

57

HART WALKED OUT into the yard after his contracts exam. His hand ached from the writing, but he felt free. What he knew about contracts was on that exam. He had left it behind.

He turned the corner of Langdell, almost skipping along, his adrenaline still pumping, things looking crisp and bright. And there, coming around the far end of the library, walking fast, was Kingsfield.

They would pass unless Hart turned away. Hart moved slightly toward the center of the path.

"Professor," Hart said, "I wanted to tell you I enjoyed your class."

Kingsfield stopped. It seemed that the professor's eyes were built in black layers, each layer obscuring the others. Without a trace of expression, Kingsfield nodded.

"Good," Kingsfield said. "That's fine."

Hart's pulse was pounding. His eyes turned into circles of feeling.

"I want to tell you that the class meant something to me," Hart said. "You meant something to me."

It was hard to tell what Kingsfield thought. He didn't reply right away. Maybe that was just because he was almost seventy years old and used to speaking to people from the lectern. Finally, the corners of his thin lips turned up in a slight smile.

"What was your name?" Kingsfield said, stepping past Hart. His voice sounded as if it came from a long way off.

"Hart, Mr. Hart," Hart said.

"Well, thank you, Mr. Hart," Kingsfield said, and then he was gone.

58

THEY WERE AT THE CAPE, tanned and healthy, sitting on the rocks above the beach, looking down into the water, sorting the mail. Hart's letters were in a small pile beside him in the sand. They hadn't been to the post office in a month because Susan said it was more fun to get the mail all at once.

The letter in Hart's hand had THE HARVARD LAW SCHOOL stamped in neat letters in the upper left-hand corner. He slipped it out of the pile and nudged it behind him.

"All right," Susan said. "You're holding out on me."

"It's my grades from the law school," he said matter-of-factly, dropping the letter on a rock.

"You know, Dad's coming down here in a week. You've never talked to him close up. Of course, it's not much of a surprise," she said. Most of her mail was advertisements. She was making them into gliders and sailing them across the beach into the water.

"I'll leave you two alone," Hart said. He picked up the letter from the law school.

"No way," Susan said.

The wind shifted behind them and her next glider caught it, sailing almost twenty yards out.

"Are you going to open the grades?" she asked, "or are you going to see if your glider will go further than mine?"

"Well," he said, "I don't know." He was thinking.

Then the wind got gusty. Hart folded the letter in half, curving up the sides, making a glider. The letters, "Harvard Law School" glistened on the wings like insignia. He stood up, tested the wind and let fly. The glider sailed up on a strong gust and then dropped down far out, landing in the waves. It held on for a while, converting into a sailboat. Finally the waves got the best of it and, waterlogged, it sank down until they could no longer see it.